Fool on the Hill

Mark Sargent

Fool on the Hill

a novel

FAST BOOKS

For my good friend,
Daniel Heagerty

Cover illustration: John Haugse
Author photo: Xeni Taze
Mountain photo: Georgiades
Much thanks to Charlotte Rubin for close reading.

FAST BOOKS are edited and published by Michael Smith
P. O. Box 1268, Silverton, OR 97381, USA
Catalog at fastbookspress.com

ISBN 978-0-9982793-4-3

1: Shamanized

The big empty isn't hard to find. On the edge of it bird song can sound a hollow note, an empty lilt. Almost a negative echo. I perched there with my eyes fixed on the eastern horizon, a jagged range of rock and pine called the Parnona. Below, patchworked with orange and olive, the Evrotas valley, and beneath my feet the Tayegetos, an ancient spine of stone that runs south toward the Mani and the sea. A hawk scribed great arcs of nothing below.

Having grown my hair out, I thought I'd try my hand at shamaning. I didn't bathe or attend myself and took to wearing raw untreated goat hides. A shepherd gave them to me, they're not used much anymore, and I fashioned from them a poncho of sorts. They stunk, but so did I. I went without my glasses, which made me squint and blink and misinterpret the distant.

A young man asked, "What about the mountain?"

"There is no mountain!" I snarled, and stomped on his foot.

He yelped and hopped about.

"There's only the ground beneath your fucking feet! Mountains, bah. When the dog crosses the river the frogs will choose sides." Cryptic is good shit. I practiced it relentlessly. "The eagle knows the turtle but the turtle knows nothing of the eagle."

I got a few extra dogs to give myself a semi-wild entourage. They loved the goat skins, I fed them well and so they worshiped the ground I walked on and obeyed my commands instantly. Okay, maybe not instantly, but close enough. This had the desired effect. People were afraid of the dogs and in awe of my command of them.

My years of observing the birds came in handy. Augury went down a bomb with the New Age types, and most villagers retain a touch of the pagan, a susceptibility to the occult, the evil eye, and Christ on a cross. A nightingale would sing and I would nod sagely and predict a birth in the next village. Hey, I didn't specify what, could be a child, could be a lamb or a chicken, though chickens don't count, birth or death, not in the village.

Time expands and contracts, it may even run backward, whatever that would entail, but we measure our mortality with our sense of it, regardless of how modern science disproves it. Perhaps it is what separates us from the rest of the species we share the planet with, this sense of time, the weight of it. But let's run time backward to the start of this venture.

Two years previous a relationship of many years had gone south; it had worn out, broken down, and left us both exhausted and in retreat. She had left no forwarding address but vanished to the West. My two adult children, after spending most of their lives in Greece, had returned to the States. The house I was in was much too large for one person, and I was adrift and didn't have the energy to consider downsizing. So I read and wrote and wandered around, alone much of the time. The odd friend visited, but most were far away, and their lives kept carrying them further. Not as a matter of geography but in the sense of time. I had stopped, somehow slipped the loop, jumped the tracks to a parallel universe so that while time was passing for me, it wasn't at the same speed as previous. I couldn't tell whether it was faster or slower, only that I wasn't in sync. This is probably not unusual for a middle-aged person living alone, especially in a situation as isolated as mine, a foreigner deep in the Greek countryside.

It also was a matter of geography. The nearest neighbor was five hundred meters away, and he was a troll who spoke no known language. Sometimes my only contact with the human world was the lights from Sparti down in the valley glittering in the darkness. And across the valley the sun kept coming up from the Parnona mountain range. Every day, and I couldn't imagine that changing anytime soon. If you needed something to worship, the sun would be a worthy object of devotion. Without it there is no life. And faith wouldn't be required, 'cause there it is, every fucking day. You can count on it.

I had money and traveled a bit, but in a dutiful way: *you have to see this and you must see that.* Why? Must the entire scorecard be completed? How far do you see from the heights of Machu Picchu? If you haven't been to Angkor Wat, will peace elude you forever? And what would this "peace" be? Convinced that there is nothing after death, conscious "forever" didn't sound very long. My hermit existence had run its course. This was my frame of mind when I decided to opt for shamaning.

No respectable shaman (respectable?) would live in my large modern pad, so I found a small stone shepherd's hut on a nearby property. There are many abandoned huts in the Lakonian countryside, remnants of a time past when flocks and herds were common in the hills and a reasonable occupation for those who didn't take to schooling. The stone shack was high on the mountain and afforded a terrific view of the valley below. I rented the property and let it become overgrown apart from a single pathway that the dogs kept well packed. I got a donkey, both as a companion and for transport: I had to haul in all my water. I named him Gurdjieff, and he ate the wild shit that was trying to take over the property. He couldn't keep up but kept the vines from slithering in the windows and strangling me in my sleep.

Gurdjieff was a jolly creature, but sometimes, without warning, he would break into a long howling bray that sounded like he was tapping into the horror of existence. He probably was. As his namesake once said, *"A man will renounce any pleasures you like but he will not give up his suffering."* We are all animals, and the vanity of homo sapiens believing they are special is really too much to bear. Species are only currents in the drift of genes, that's what Darwin said and nobody has proved him wrong. Knowing that the human mind serves evolutionary success rather than truth gives one the illusion of liberation. That's all we get, that tart illusion, that fragment of imagination. Someday homo sapiens will be gone, and the earth will hardly notice that this brief moment has passed.

In the hut I had a gas burner, a wood stove, and some oil lamps. It wasn't that rough, but in the light of a lamp at night it appeared primitive and mysterious. I fashioned a couple of crude masks and hung them on the wall along with the collection of rudimentary tools I allowed myself. Bundles of wild herbs hung from a crude shelf. I had a couple of hand drums, a penny whistle and, my soul indulgence, an alto saxophone. Simple, Spartan, that is what I was going for. Along the path to the hut were mobiles cum wind chimes made with goat bells. And several small statues: a Buddha, a dancing Shiva, a Ganesh. Flawed mandalas dangled from trees or peeked from tree hollows or cracks in the rock. The whole setup looked great, and by the time visitors had reached the hut, accompanied by five dogs and welcomed by the braying Gurdjieff, they were ready for anything I laid on them. It's called softening the imagination. I hesitate to use the word consciousness, which is given too much credit, when it is the unconscious mind that is making most of our "choices."

Once or twice a month I would saddle up Gurdjieff and ride down to the village accompanied by the dogs. It took an hour to get there. I had large plastic containers for water. First two or three times we stopped traffic, all conversation at cafés ceased, mothers grabbed their children, and the village dogs went berserk. Then the villagers realized it was me and returned to their coffees, nodding to each other and tapping their heads: *Max, he's gone mad, or something. Too much living by himself up there. He should get himself a new woman.* Sometimes a shepherd would try and make this point, but I would answer: *An enforced solitude is hell, a voluntary one heaven.* They still thought I was mad. And to be sure my solitude was a mix of the voluntary and the enforced. I'd lash the water, great sacks of dog food, and whatever provisions I required onto Gurdjieff and back up we'd go. I walked on the way back.

Shamaning is a social activity, otherwise you're just a hermit. I'd done hermiting, so I needed some acolytes, I hesitate to say followers, let's call them spiritual companions, fellow travelers on the path, but needy, of something. And who isn't? I contacted a small select group of friends from my previous life in the States and informed them that I had gone into the shaman game. They all found this a great idea, two of them asked why it had taken me so long to take this up, and they began leaving anonymous reports on specific internet exchanges concerning a holy fool somewhere in the mountains above Sparti. Note, I did not involve my adult children, who were also living in America. The shaman gig was something I didn't mention to them because they thought I had already dropped too far out. I mean, why would anyone voluntarily live in a hut without water? Though after a couple of weeks I decided a weekly shower wouldn't dent my shaman cred.

It took a while, but eventually folks, most under the age of thirty, began to make their way up the mountain. The first were a German couple. I heard the dogs long before I saw them. They loved visitors and would bark and bound about while leading them to the hut. Wolfgang and Pia, they were glowing and dreadlocked, pierced and golden and laden with expensive backpacks and camping equipment. Folks from the German world, Swizz, Austrians, and those from the Fatherland, usually have excellent kit. I was sitting out front cleaning some wild greens—timing is everything. Gurdjieff started to bray.

I shouted at him, "Gurdjieff, chill man. You've done your bit." They turned and stared at Gurdjieff, who was a free-range donkey and coming toward them. He sniffed, nudged their backpacks with his nose, snorted.

"Looks like he approves of you. Take your backpacks off. And dogs, enough already, beasts cease!" The dogs quieted down and came and arrayed themselves at my feet. I was still sitting, still cleaning *horta*. Wolfgang and Pia dropped their bags and stood stretching out their shoulders. They approached.

"Good morning. I'm Wolfgang and this is Pia. Are you Teiresias?"

Dig my shaman handle: Teiresias, he who delights in signs, the ancient blind soothsayer of Greek mythology and the only one from the myths who had been both a man and a woman. I looked up from my seat on a chunk of wood into their beautiful blue eyes. "Sometimes." I put down my knife and reached up toward them. They got the cue; each grabbed a hand and pulled me to my feet. I gave each of them a robust hug. I was making this shit up as I went along but I didn't get the impression they were about to prostrate themselves, and was grateful for that. I believe there's a big difference between the guru, holy man type, and shaman, holy fool, cosmic jester. I was shooting for the latter, which appeared to allow a broad spectrum of activity, a figure oddly related to a common character in the Greek countryside, the village idiot. Mad or wise? Is that shepherd boy as dull as he looks, or enlightened? Who knows? Ha ha. Also, gurus generally require a bit of devotion somewhere along the line. I didn't want any part of that. That sounds like they won't go away, you can't get rid of them, along with a lot of bowing and scraping. All this inevitably leads to rivalry and intrigue among the faithful. Nah, fuck that shit.

That brings up the question, what did I want out of shamaning? "Shamaning," it sounds like something you do to the carpet, or your car. I'm having the Buick shamaned today. I can't meet you tomorrow, the shamanizers are coming. *"Yes sir, we have you signed up for 'The Full Shaman.' You know, for another fifty bucks we'll enlightenize all the windows on the first floor."* Where do I fucking sign? Give it to me! I want it all. But, of course, that was hardly the case. I was living in a hut in the mountains of southern Greece, which was a long way from having it all, or very close, depending on your relationship with desire and its satisfaction. Mostly, I just wanted the odd visitors, but ones that were curious and aggressively following their curiosity. Which brings up the question of free will, but we'll get to that later.

So I'm standing there with Wolfgang and Pia, and they are staring at me, waiting for a sign that maybe I know something they don't. Do I?

"How did you get here?" I asked.

Wolfgang looked at his feet. "We walked."

"You walked? From where? All the way from Deutschland?" The accent gave them away.

"No, no, from Sparti."

"That's still a serious walk. You must have left at dawn. I don't do anything at dawn anymore, unless I'm already doing it. You dig what I'm saying? Anyway, sit down and give it a rest. These short rounds of wood make good chairs, or just get on the earth, as you please." Without moving but just folding her legs, Pia slowly sank to the ground. It was a very graceful gesture. Wolfgang grabbed a chunk of wood. I left them there and entered the hut to make a pot of tea.

While putting on water to boil I considered what to do next. Something unexpected but comforting. I brought out the teapot and cups and set them on a makeshift table near the door. Then I sank to my knees in front of Pia and unlaced her sturdy hiking boots, pulled them off and then the socks. I gave each foot a short vigorous massage. I suddenly remembered John Travolta and Samuel Jackson discussing foot massage in "Pulp Fiction" and almost laughed out loud. By their clothes and style I figured they'd already done Asia, or some of it. I took a flyer. "When were you in India?"

Pia, already softened up by the foot massage, gave me a blissful smile. "We were there last year. How did you know?"

"See the crow up there in that oak tree. That's Langston. He was sure you had been." Langston squawked on cue. "Yeah, yeah, you are the chillest crow on the mountain." He jumped off the branch, stroked his wings once, and glided to the hut roof. We all watched him. "Now you might ask, what the fuck does a bird know? Who knows? But remember, crow is the smartest creature in the air. How does the mind of bird work? I assume differently than us and try and listen. It's all guesswork, of course, but you know, the more you listen to them, spend time with them, the more sense they make. Projection, more than likely, but I'm comfortable with mystery. Or ignorance." I moved to Wolfgang and repeated the foot attention. "Sometimes it feels like he's just telling jokes, which I don't get, of course, though I laugh along with him, especially when he's got an audience of crows. Perch comedy."

Pia pointed toward Langston, "What kind of crow is it?"

"He's a hooded crow. Looks like he's in formal evening wear with the grey body and everything else black."

"Oh yes, we have that bird in Germany. He's called a *Nebelkrähe*, mist crow."

"Langston, did you hear that? *Nebelkrähe*. Mist crow, I like it." I had noticed a map in Wolfgang's jacket pocket, a guide to the European hiking trail that ran south down the spine of the Tayegetos. These were very expensive hiking boots they were wearing. I made another guess. "Are you hiking the trail?"

Wolfgang nodded with a smile. "We came down into Tripi and walked into Sparti. The trail is somewhere above you, isn't it?"

"'Further up and further in,' as Mr. Lewis had it." Hmm, the Christian apologist drew blanks, wrong cultural reference. I tried a bit of Rilke.

"Einsam steigt er dahin, in die Berge des Urleids."

They excused my pronunciation and nodded in recognition, regardless of how inappropriate the quote. "Alone, he climbs to the mountains of primal pain."

"I can lead you to it."

Wolf and Pia grinned and gave each other a knowing look. So far so wise.

I heard a jackdaw and raised my head and listened to the *chaka chaka chack.* "That's a jackdaw. He's part of the crow family. He's called *kavka* in Czech, Kafka. There he is."

And it worked out. They pitched a tent, the dogs wanted to help and made it really difficult, we built a fire, roasted some spuds, ate some walnuts, boiled the wild greens I had cleaned and some cheese I had hanging in a goat skin and a jug of wine Gangman and P. brought. Of course it worked. I had welcomed them with a foot massage, the dogs were at their charming best, we sat around the fire in a crisp October night, Milky Way swarming overhead, drinking wine and talking the talk that people of experience can who know they will never see each other again. They were both bright, well read, and very articulate in English. During their time in India they had specifically sought out holy men. In Varanasi they had met Ali Das Baba, who had managed to funnel what sounded like an overload of energy into Wolfgang, bang. "He touched my head and looked into my eyes. His eyes were glowing with light and I started shaking, like epilepsy or something. Then it felt like I was floating, that I had left earth. Pure energy was flowing through me and everything was a white light. That's what it was like."

"Cool. Sounds terrific. How long did this experience last?"

"I couldn't tell. Pia said it was about ten minutes."

"Ya, that's about right."

"You called this energy 'pure.' Why? I mean, how do you tell?"

"I don't know. I just knew it." Wolfgang shrugged.

I threw another round of wood on the fire. "And what happened afterward, after the white light and the pure energy?"

"Pia helped me back to our room and I slept for twenty-four hours."

"And then?"

"For the next two weeks I had extra sensitivity. I was aware of the energy flowing through everything. Sometimes I could see it. It was as though the living world was communicating with me. I could understand the trees; I could read the minds of dogs and birds, though not other humans. I could see and feel the energy flowing through them too, I just couldn't read their minds. Then I got sick, dysentery, and was very sick for about ten days. By the time that was over I was back to my normal self, a German in India. What I want to know is, how do I get back to that?"

"Fantastic story, Wolfgang. It sounds like you were ready for the experience, to receive the energy or teaching or whatever Ali Das Baba gave you, but not prepared to use it, or remain in that semi-enlightened state. The Buddhists would say that you couldn't stay with it because you had no practice, no process that would allow you to build on this flash, this epiphany, this satoric shazam. And when they say practice, they mean meditation, essentially."

"But what do you think?"

"We'll get to that. *Seegah, seegah*, slowly, slowly, as they say here." I picked up a rope and began to knot it. "There was this famous Buddhist teacher about a thousand years ago named Tilopa. Before he was enlightened he worked as a pimp and a bouncer at a brothel at night, shades of Malcolm X, and during the day he ground sesame seeds. He's mostly remembered because he had a famous student, Naropa. Naropa had an aristocratic background and was renowned throughout India as the master of Buddhist texts. Then one day an old hag told him he didn't know shit and should seek out Tilopa, who did. After a long search he found him, but Tilopa ignored him for a long time. He eventually put him through twelve trials, most of which resulted in Naropa being beaten nearly to death. After each, Tilopa would magically restore him to health. It was all about breaking down Naropa's attachment and vanity. It is often the case in enlightenment stories that the seeker is subjected to drastic trials. Would a modern pilgrim put up with it? Now you pay the money and they give you an enlightenment certificate.

Tilopa gave Naropa six words of advice, or six nails of key points, if you want the literal translation. These are single words, but we need a few more. *Mi-mno*: don't recall, in other words, let go of the past. *Mi-bsam*: don't imagine, let go of the idea of the future." I tried to tie a knot for each precept. "*Mi-sems*: which means, don't think, let go of the present, of your ideas about what is happening. *Mi-dpyod:* don't examine, stop trying to figure anything out. *Mi-sgom:* don't control, let go of the vanity of trying to make anything happen." Our faces glowed golden in the firelight. The dogs snored about our feet. Nocturnal birds called through the dark. "This is an old rope trick Henry Crow Dog taught me. He was an old Ogala Lakota medicine man, and I was staying at his place in the Black Hills during the Wounded Knee occupation. That was forty years ago. Crow Dog was part of a long line of medicine men. His son, Leonard Crow Dog, is an important spiritual leader for Indigenous peoples. Back in America."

"That's only five." Wolfgang had been counting.

"You're right. Here, take this end of the rope. The sixth word is *rang-sar-bzhag*, relax. Chill, rest. Pull the rope." Wolfgang gave the rope a good tug and all the knots disappeared. It was good trick. Flies could have flown in their mouths, they were in full gawk. I laughed. Wolfgang was nodding his head, the story wasn't lost on him. Pia was grinning and rocking back and forth.

"On that note I'm going to let go of conscious mind and enter the land of nod." I stood up. "Relax, let go, let the body take over. Mañana, my friends."

In the morning we had paxamadi, twice-baked bread that you revive with water and olive oil, a sprinkle of oregano, and voilà. Some pears and lots of tea. Then they broke camp and were about to hoist their packs when I stopped them.

"Wait, wait, here, let Gurdjieff carry your packs till you hit the trail. It's easy for him, and he likes to carry a load once in a while. You know, keep in touch with his inner beast of burden." Wolfgang and Pia were ready to be amused, and we lashed their backpacks to Gurdjieff. "Hey, you know, I think I'll say '*yasou* and *kalo taxidi*' here. Gurdjieff knows the way. It's only twenty minutes. The dogs will go too. There are signs, and anyway, how lost can you get? No matter where you go, you're still on the mountain. When you find the trail just slap him on the ass and he'll come back. The dogs may walk with you a while, but they'll come back. Or maybe one of them will decide she needs a new human." I shrugged. "They can come and go as they please."

Pia locked me in a bear hug, kissed me on the lips, and winked with a grin. Wolfgang was next. "Thank you, for everything."

"And nothing," I added. "Wolfgang, as they say, drop everything, except maybe her. I'd keep her close, but detached."

They walked off up the trail. Gurdjieff wanted to lead, but the dogs were having none of it and ran ahead barking their fucking heads off. I watched till they disappeared. I looked up at Langston on his oak perch. "Well, zippity doo dah, Langston. I do believe we're in the game."

"Kraa, kraa, kraa."

2: Swamp Gas

"The art of losing isn't hard to master." —Elizabeth Bishop

In language acquisition, talking to oneself comes after talking to others, and the octopus can adapt to colors it cannot see. I had plenty of time to converse with myself while slowly becoming indistinguishable from the landscape. Aloneness is a key factor in even pretending to be a shaman, especially deliberate solitude. The more time you spend by yourself the more ludicrous the follies of humankind appear. And let's face it, all is folly—which, obviously, fits right in with being a faux shaman. Robert Wright wrote, "We deceive ourselves in order to deceive others better." So, for instance, the best liar is the one who believes his lie.

I had no desire to bullshit anyone, though of course that was inevitable. So I kept up with my reading. Every week I'd trek over to my house and exchange texts. I thought having lots of books in the hut gave the wrong impression. The attraction of the shaman is that he's the embodiment of the natural law, of experience outside of the written word, handed down by generations of shamans, the wild who listen to birds and commune with reptiles. I didn't have the benefit of that experience and hadn't learned a thing from lizards, so I kept up my studies because, while I certainly couldn't believe my shaman subterfuge, if I could pass on whatever I had culled from my studies and observations of the world, why not?

And let's face it, most folks don't give a thought to the *what* and *why* of existence. Why should they? You live the life, or you don't. You get up, you go to work. Maybe you have a child and try to raise it, more than likely making all the same errors your parents did. The idea of human progress is nonsense, we cannot remake the world. Given what we know of life on this planet, our species is here for just a short while. But we can strive to see it clearly, though this certainly has nothing to do with happiness. Chickens with leg injuries will choose a feed they don't normally favor if it is laced with a painkiller.

I had a vision."

"Yeah."

She looked at me with a mix of astonishment and annoyance. "Didn't you hear me? I said I had a vision."

People spend so much time watching themselves and it fills them with self-importance. And really, one person's vision is another person's headache. As with most everything else, it depends on what you invest in it. "What do you mean by that?"

"Don't *you* know?"

Perhaps I should put a sign down at the beginning of the trail: *Faux Shaman up ahead. Leave your expectations here.* "Aha, right, but 'vision,' that's too vague. I most definitely do not know what *you* mean by that word. Tell me about it." I stroked Voltaire's head.

Monique, a thirty-seven-year-old social worker cum art therapist from Quebec, squirmed on her log chair. Folks can spend years pursuing a flawed idea but upon realizing the fallacy of their endeavor want instant clarity. Say you've got some fishing line and everyday you unravel more of it and entangle and knot it, and you do this for months till you have one great ball of thin translucent line. You wouldn't expect someone to able to untangle it instantly. That's a half-arrived metaphor, but the impatience of those who seek answers is, to some extent, the energy that drives their search.

"It was a gray afternoon and I was loading pots into the kiln. There wasn't anyone else in the studio and I had some Bach on the radio. And I dropped a large, beautiful bowl, one of the best things I've ever done. And I don't drop things. I'm not clumsy. And when I looked down on the broken shards I saw his face and he was calling to me."

I wanted to ask who but assumed we'd get to that.

"There was no question about the meaning. He was calling me to him. He was reaching around the planet and tugging at my heart. He was saying we belong together and now is the time. His need rose into me. I could see it as though it was written on the floor. And I knew, instantly, what I must do."

"I'm right with ya. Who did you see and what did he compel you to do?"

"It was Pieter! Of course it was Pieter!" She threw her hands up in the air.

"Who is Pieter?"

"You mean you don't know?" Monique was incredulous.

"No. I don't know. How would I?"

"Well, I just assumed you would. You know, reading the vibrations or whatever it is your type do."

"I don't know what you've heard about me, but let me assure you that I don't read minds. As far as vibrations go, eh, sometimes I get a sense of them, just like most everybody else. But if you want a seer, you've walked up the wrong mountain."

This news deflated her a bit. She plunged on.

"Perhaps I did, but I'm here and there's nobody else to talk to." She looked around to confirm this. Gurdjieff did that exhalation/shaking of the lips thing donkeys do. Langston laughed one note. The dogs sighed in their sleep. "By the way, what do I call you? Teiresias, that's a bit much."

"You can call me Ray." An old joke from my childhood, lost on Monique.

"Ray? Whatever. Pieter is an artist. A sculptor and painter, a master of space and form and color."

"Great, where is he now?" I was hoping he was still alive, 'cause I don't know shit about summoning the dead and we didn't have enough for a seance, unless we could somehow get the dogs involved.

"He's in Monemvasia."

"Monique, I'm lost here. Let's go back to the broken bowl. I'm missing too much detail to make sense of it. Tell me the whole story. We've got lots of time."

She took a big breath. "So within the shards of my broken bowl I saw Pieter, and he was calling me to him. You see, early this year I met Pieter Van Houven at an exhibit in Montreal. It was a large solo show, and as I walked around the galleries I could feel the paintings in my gut. It was a body experience. It was as though the oil and pigment were coming off the canvases and wrapping around me. And then I met *him*." Another deep breath. "We bonded instantly. We were old souls who had seen much and traveled far to reach this moment."

I was already feeling bad for Monique. I had heard

this story before, and while sometimes it played out on gentle seas, there were considerably more shipwrecks and drownings than safe harbors.

"We spent the next week together, 24-7, we never parted, always we were touching, caressing, speaking from the very bottom of our beings. We crossed universes of passion. He's a great artist, and he told me I would be his new muse, the muse of the last third of his life."

"How old is he?"

"Fifty-five. About your age, I would think."

"That's true."

"The age difference meant nothing. Eighteen years is not a significant amount of time. Our souls were ancient and ageless. Many lifetimes had come and gone so that we would finally meet. And the union of our bodies, my god, never have I given and received such love, such tensile articulation to the breaking point but never breaking, never breaking but always flowing back to the center, to the sacral chakra. There we burned, but our fuel was never exhausted."

"Fantastic. Everyone should have those experiences, but many don't, I suppose."

"Not what we had. Ours was unique. But then he had to leave. He had a show opening in London. We agreed that he would send word when I should come. I'm not naïve." I didn't allow even a whisper of a smile. "I know a man such as this has other women in his life. I realized that it would take some time to sort things out. A few weeks, or even months, are meaningless when you share what we had."

"Did he send for you?"

"Well yes, as I told you, through the broken vase."

"Just that?"

"Yes, I know how it sounds now, but I was utterly convinced that he was speaking to me through this accident. There was no way to contact him. He doesn't use a phone. You have to go through his agent in London, but I didn't need that. I quit my job, rented my apartment, and flew to Athens. There I caught a bus to Monemvasia."

"No hesitation."

"None."

"Damn. Let's take a break, Monique. How about we take a walk? The dogs will come along. They love it. And so do I."

I had a fine fire flaming away. Monique had brought a few things to eat, and we fashioned a meal from them. During the walk I had been trying to get a grip on Monique's story. That she had altered her life dramatically due to a "vision," though it wasn't really the vision so much as the experience that led to the need for the vision, still, it was a bold statement for someone of her experience. By that I mean, people in their early twenties, late teens, do this sort of thing regularly, or should, but to be mature and still be ready to drop everything meant, well, what did it mean? Boredom is the word that came to mind: in the midst of a dreary winter I found a light and heat. But it can't be that simple. She was single, and alone, which makes it less complicated. It makes it easier to be reckless if you don't have someone to bounce your craziness off, no one to call bullshit, no one to say *you are out of your fucking mind!*

"Sometime on that long bus ride I began to question what I was doing. I know, that's a bit late, but until then my passion, the energy personified by the vision, kept me pushing forward. All I could think of was wrapping my arms around him, describing the people I had seen on the journey. I even took notes. I even looked forward to sharing his cigarettes, Gitanes, and I don't smoke. I was mad with love. When I arrived in Monemvasia it was early afternoon, and I walked out to the rock. You've been there, of course?"

I nodded. "Many times."

"It has a beautiful magic. I asked a couple of shopkeepers where his studio was. They knew him, and it was quite easy to find. While walking through the village I bought a chilled bottle of champagne. It's a very touristy place, isn't it?"

"Yes, it is."

"I arrived at his doorstep, flushed, breathing hard from the walk, bag on my back, bubbly gripped in my hand, and knocked on the old wooden door. I heard someone inside shout something in Greek, I felt like singing, and then the door swung open." She sighed. "And instead of flinging myself into Pieter's arms I was reaching out my hand and trying to introduce myself to a beautiful twenty-something Greek girl who was giving me a very suspicious stare. I didn't look like a spontaneous art patron."

If you didn't see this coming I would suggest you don't leave the house without a chaperone or a well-trained dog.

"I must have turned pale. It was like hearing that my father had died in an automobile accident. Loss, total loss. I dropped the champagne, which miraculously didn't break, and staggered and grabbed for the door frame. The weight of my backpack was suddenly pulling me down. The young woman, Calliope is her name, tried to support me but we were struggling, and then, there was Pieter. And he

wrapped us up in his arms and we were no longer falling."
Monique stared into the fire. Everything has more impact
by firelight.

"Well, the situation was obvious. She was not the
housekeeper, or at least that wasn't all she was. They were
kind, and gracious, and why not? They weren't the one
mortified by embarrassment. They were embarrassed for
me. They hadn't gambled everything. They hadn't had the
great love of their life exposed as a fantasy, a ridiculous
projection. No, they made tea. They had a balcony that
overlooked the sea. We looked at some of the new work.
They even invited me to stay, but I couldn't imagine staying
there knowing that somewhere else in the house they were
together. They finally invented some pretense, an errand
for Calliope. She was stunning, by the way, a great mane
of swirling black hair and a profile like she'd stepped off a
fresco in Santorini or Knossos. You imagine ships being
launched to pursue her. What had I been thinking?

"Pieter apologized, asked for my forgiveness.
Forgiveness, my god, as if life was so easy. *'Sorry. I didn't
really mean to cut your heart out.'* And yet, he was sorry, I think.
He hadn't expected me to show up at his door thinking
we'd take up where we left off. It was a week-long fling
in a faraway city. He probably has them regularly and then
returns to that year's Calliope. We drank the champagne
and slowly went over that week in Montreal. As we did I
got the sinking feeling that much of it was my doing, my
reading into it what I was so desperate to have happen.
What a mad, love-struck fool I had been, like some fifteen-
year-old slapped sick by her first boy, her first lay. I didn't
for a moment stop and ask myself, what are you doing? No,
I was playing grand opera, and Pieter was willing to sing

along. Why wouldn't he? He had a ticket out of town.

"Calliope returned. They wanted me to stay for lunch but I couldn't. I was too ashamed of myself, and now that the energy of my passion had been scattered, the fatigue of the trip was really hitting me. But mostly, I was devastated. I had bet everything, gladly, and now I had nothing. I thanked them, said goodbye, took one last look around the house—beautiful, out of a magazine, just as I had imagined it—and walked out.

I found a café, ordered a coffee, and waited for my being to coalesce, to come back together. For something to fill the utterly empty shell I was. It was mid-afternoon, the place was empty. My god, what a fucking cliché! How did I become this banal? This pathetic? I must have been radiating despair, because the woman who served me made herself a coffee, sat down at my table, and asked after me. I gave her the short version. I left out the names. She probably guessed who I was talking about but was kind enough not to say. She asked what I was going to do, and I told her I hadn't the faintest idea. She called a friend who had rooms. She came to the café and took me back to this tiny hotel she had. She fed me lunch, and that night, along with the woman from the café, we drank wine until very late. And they actually made me laugh."

"Sisterhood in a time of need."

Monique gave a short laugh. "Sometimes it's the only thing that will do. But in the morning I felt just as bad, just as crushed. That's when Cassandra, the woman with the hotel, mentioned you. She said she knew you."

"Yeah, I've known Cassandra for years. A very kind person."

"Yes, she is. Anyway, she suggested I pay you a visit. I

mean, I didn't have anywhere else to go. She said you had interesting things to say sometimes."

"Sometimes," I laughed, "when you have nowhere else to go. And here you are."

Monique nodded and poked the fire. I pulled out the pipe and loaded it up. Every year a generous and enterprising shepherd who works these hills gave me a bag of cannabis. He grew it in an isolated place not too far from my hut. He knew I knew but didn't disturb it, didn't rat him out, and so, as a gesture of solidarity between us who knew the mountain, he made me a gift, which greatly exceeded my needs. Monique was amenable.

B ut why?" Monique asked. "Isn't following your vision a cliché? Doesn't pop culture hold this up as the romantic ideal? Isn't it all part of the same bullshit? Why the fuck was I so needy and stupid?"

"Why? I don't know about that. I'm not too good with 'why.' Let's try and see where we are now. I want you to take this piece of paper and this pen and write down everything that is troubling you and what you expected before coming up here. It could be one word, it could be paragraphs. Length doesn't matter, just try and put down anything you might have anticipated or prepared yourself for. Whatever you think you're carrying around. Writing things down is good exercise. It's a different type of memory, of consideration."

She scribbled away, covering one side of the paper and half the other with a fine small script. Monique was nothing if not thorough. She stopped and looked up from the paper, her eyes glowing.

"Done?"

She nodded.

"Sign and date it."

She followed instructions.

"Okay, now make a ball of it."

She cocked her head quizzically.

"Yeah, just wad it up, into a sphere, if you will. Like the planet we're on."

She scrunched it up and then looked back at me.

"Throw it in the fire."

"What? You mean you aren't even going to read it?"

"Nah, it's your stuff. I can't do anything with it. Throw it away, but before you do that, read it again."

Monique stared at the ball of paper in her hand, flexing and releasing her grip. "I don't need to reread it." Then she nodded to herself and threw the ball into the fire. It flared for a moment and vanished.

I slapped my hands together. "Great. It's time for the sweat." Early in my faux-shaman adventure I had built a small sweat lodge out of bamboo and then covered it with the tarps we use to collect the olives. I had an old tin *tapsee*, a low, round, handleless pan, dug in in the middle for the rocks. I fished the rocks out of the fire with a set of giant tongs, placed them in a metal bucket. "Monique, could you grab that jug of water and follow me?" The sweat lodge was maybe twenty meters away but you couldn't see it from the hut. "Here, you can hang your clothes on this tree." We got in, I closed up the opening and hit the rocks with the water. The first waves of steam are really intense. In seconds the sweat was pouring off of me. We were sitting across from each other in a small utterly black intensely hot space. The other's presence is powerfully felt.

"Ray?"

"Yes."

"I'm no longer young, on the cusp of middle age. Was this the last romance? The last time I'm going to feel this way?"

"Well, yes, in one way it is. You can't repeat anything. So certainly, you are never going to go through *that* experience again. You've done it. You've proved yourself capable of taking enormous risks, of not clinging to all the dull rewards of the bourgeois life but jumping. Sure, it was obsessive, but in the end all you did was bruise yourself up real bad. This may make you wiser. Or it won't."

"Do you believe in love?" Damn. If I was charging for this you could say that Monique intended to get her money's worth.

I took a deep breath and exhaled noisily. "A pointed question penetrates the darkness. I suppose you're talking about romantic love. To begin, let me ask another question, and really, I ask this of myself. Do you need to believe in something to experience it? I have felt and acted in a way that I described as love: that all-encompassing glow, the obsessive consideration of the object of love, the nothing-is-more-important bliss that can accompany this feeling, this elemental surge that seems to reach every cell. But, and this is a big but, the way we react to this feeling, the process that allows us to fashion it into something that we can describe, depends entirely on the language and narratives our societies create, these images we all use because that's how you talk about love. Thank you, Ray Carver. Can we separate all the expectations the culture has seduced us with? So yes, I believe I have experienced romantic love on several occasions, and I mean as an adult. But I'm suspicious of it, our sense of it is so corrupted. It might just be chemical reactions that we have no control over? On the other hand, you could make an argument that it serves evolutionary success, bringing the sexes together long enough to reproduce. That's part of it—'long enough'—it's temporary. It doesn't linger too long. Like smoke, or mist, or let's borrow one from the UFO debunkers, swamp gas. Romantic love is like swamp gas, you think the universe has intervened on your behalf." I threw some water on the rocks and the blackness exploded in steam.

"Stop, you don't need to go any further. I know what you're going to say."

"Really?" Amazing, because I didn't know where I was going with this riff.

"Yes, it's fucking obvious. Christ, I didn't need to come up here to realize that!"

"I'm sure that's the case." It usually is, but what's the revelation?

"I tried to hang on to it. He left it at the departure gate. I so wanted to will it to live. To nurture it like some fucking plant. What a moron!"

Oh, that's what she's rocking. That wasn't where I was going, I think, but sure, why not? "It's generally experienced by the young for a reason." Wow, Teiresias, that's really fucking wildly true. How trite can you get. My brain was poached.

"Maybe, except I was ready for it. But the energy of that type of encounter shuts off part of your brain. Rational mind or something? Your equilibrium thing, balance. You lose track of it."

"It requires a wee bit of detachment. Or maybe an alarm clock that rings every . . . two weeks, then the next time, say six weeks. And then again. The idea being that

27

at some point you'll stop and ask, What's the alarm for?"

"I didn't even get that long. I mean, I knew it. I knew when he was leaving, but I was already projecting myself into that house in Monemvasia. I was already indispensable to him. My life was changing forever."

"It did." I find that twenty to thirty minutes is enough for the sweat. There are Native American groups that do sessions for hours, but really, a half is fine. "Let's get out of here."

We were wrapped in blankets by the fire.

"So what should I do?" Monique was relentless.

"You're asking me?"

"Well yes, isn't that what people do? They hike up here and ask the question."

"Sure, that happens. But most come here to tell a story. And I listen, and then they go back down."

"That's it?"

"Often. And okay, I respond to their story, and sometimes I tell a story. We're storytelling creatures. We seek a narrative. And there's a certain formality at play that helps create a vivid atmosphere. You come up here to tell your story. Did you take a cab as far as the road goes?"

Monique nodded. "Yeah, I did."

"Cool. Why not? But it's still a journey of sorts, you go out of your way. You make an effort. You know, I don't get any Syrian refugees up here. We have the privilege of believing our story is important."

"It is."

"But not *more*. That's the crux of it. We have halted for a moment to consider our feelings. How exquisitely decadent."

Monique was moving on. "I think I'll go to France, Southern France. French is my mother tongue. I have skills. Something new, maybe Provence?"

"The Mediterranean is always a good idea."

"You don't really do anything, do you?"

"Oh fuck, are you going to expose me to the world?"

"It will go viral," she laughed, "no one will visit."

"Is that a threat, or a promise?"

I sank into my mattress. I find the whole process exhausting, even not doing anything. I was asleep within minutes. Later I felt a weight on the mattress. I was only half awake, and the body next to mine was warm. Monique caressed me to attention, straddled me, and impaled herself. There was a moon, and its light cut through the window and illuminated her, backlit her so that she was edged in a soft silver sheen, and she rode me slow and easy into deeper night.

Langston kraa-kraacking away sounded like he was lecturing the dogs. Generally I sleep well, and this night was no exception, I was completely restored. I stood up and opened the door. Lakonia curved and bent away, thousands of acres of olive trees marching over the hills and flooding the valley. The tent we had set up last night for Monique sat neatly folded by the door. It was about eight and the whole world was turning toward the sun. I stepped out and stretched and looked at the gathering of animals. The dogs were front and center, eager for a stroke, Gurdjieff on the perimeter, as is his nature, Langston still squawking, and Pasolini, my old tom, was sitting in the doorway.

"*Kalimera*, gang. I trust y'all slept well. I certainly did.

But tell me, when did Monique leave? Did you guys walk her down to the road? At least?" The dogs milled about, noncommittal. The ignorance of the pack. I summoned Stein, the smartest of the dogs. I had tried calling her Gertrude, but it didn't take, she just wasn't a Gertrude, but Stein worked right away. My experience with dogs and cats has led me to believe that in most cases the females are smarter. "Stein, when did she split? Did she leave anything?" Langston started up again. Stein trotted over to the woodpile. I followed and there, pinned to the chopping block with a hatchet, was a piece of paper. I freed the paper. Just a few words. Bravo, Monique. She had quoted a seminal Taoist text on, if you will, your personal footprint.

> *Gone, gone without*
> *leaving a trace.*

And at the bottom of the page, *Burn this.*

3: Darkness and the rest

"We are hard-wired for the illusion of self." — *John Gray*

Morning again. The sun was struggling to break through a low cloudbank that clung to the Parnona. Rays of orange were flaring as though the mountain range was on fire. The dogs were milling about, having risen to their feet upon my appearance. Songbirds were twittering through the trees. Langston started squawking.

"Damn, Langston, there's nothing even vaguely melodic about that yack coming outta you, is there?" I put my hand up. "I know, we live the life available. I can't, for instance, fly. But I can write the odd poem, and I have scribed one for you." I produced a page from my back pocket. "I have a possible title, but I'm not convinced. It's 'Would You Like Mustard with That?' Doesn't exactly grab you where you live. But the poem itself is all right. Hell, it's a fucking sonnet." I straightened out the page, glanced at the dogs and looked up at Langston. "All right, check it out, gang. Your human is putting down the verse."

I believe a deal was made,
between the family crow and god,
they'd be the smartest of all fowl
but no music ever would they make.

And so, reduced to commentary,
they squawk and talk among themselves,

superior in conception, prone to complaint,
addicted to dazzle and light.

There was one other gift the god bestowed
on all the members of the clan of crow,
raven, magpie, jackdaw, rook,
no matter how, raw or cooked,
there's just no way to take this meat,
for crow's impossible to eat.

"You can hold the applause, not necessary, nor, in the case of y'all, even possible." Gurdjieff had turned away during my recitation. "Gurdjieff, what's up? You don't dig my po?" He turned his head and looked back at me and then let loose with a load of shit. "Whoa, dude, that's harsh. Okay, okay, next time I'll write a guy-THOO-ree (donkey) poem. Nobility of the beast and all that. I promise. Damn." He snorted and clomped over to his water bucket and noisily drank.

It was late morning and I was fixing the gutters on the roof, trying to make my water catchment a bit more efficient. A minor adjustment only, when the dogs suddenly perked up, and then Stein ran off down the path and the rest followed. Three minutes later I could hear them barking, but not with aggression. Eventually up the path walked Stavros, playing with the dogs, punching and throwing them about while they yelped with delight.

Stavros lived in the nearby village and lived a life I thought of as typical of a native male in the countryside, which was, essentially, a little of this, a little of that. He had five hundred olive trees which he tended, and although unlicensed, he could wire a house, build a stone wall, and service your truck. It was the only way to survive in the country, have a multiplicity of skills and be prepared to use them. Farming wasn't nearly enough. A visit from Stavros was a pleasant surprise.

"Yo Stavro," I yelled while descending the ladder, "*Ti kanis, sýn-tro-fo mou?*" (How are you, my comrade?)

He hung his head. "Not so good, Max, not so good." The villagers, of course, didn't use my stage name.

"What's dragging you down, brother?"

"It's my Penelope. She's not good. She's getting worse."

I put out a bottle of local raki (we call it *tsipuro*), glasses, and some walnuts. "Sit down, tell me what's happening."

"She's very depressed, hardly speaks, never leaves the house. It's like a dark cloud has descended over our home. I don't know what to do."

"You've taken her to the doctors in Sparti?"

"Oh, they're worthless. They just write out prescriptions. Pills that don't work. I took her to Athens as well. They're no better up there."

"What do they say it is?"

"Depression. The village idiot could have told me that. He did, as a matter of fact. And the Papas, he's worthless. Comes by once a week, but all he wants is money."

"Just depression?"

"Sometimes they throw out terms like bipolar. I've read up on it. If she's bipolar, when is coming the mania part? We could use a little mania. Nothing they have done has helped, not even a little bit." He held up his hand, thumb against his forefinger, a country gesture for a small amount.

"I believe depression can be very hard to treat. I don't know anything about it, really. Sometimes you have to see a lot of doctors before you get one that can help. As far as I understand, it is often a case of chemistry amiss."

"Chemistry. Can you come and take a look?" He was twisting his hat in his hands.

"Me? Like I just said, I don't know anything about this sort of thing."

"But you know a lot. You read and talk to lots of people. I'm sure you help some of them, too."

"Stavro, I listen to the petty little problems of the bourgeoisie. It's often just part of their holiday. You're talking about the big darkness here. I can't penetrate that. I wouldn't know where to begin."

"Max, please. Do this for me. I have nowhere else to turn."

Wow, that's a bleak prospect. "Sure, of course, my friend. Let's go."

Down the trail I tried to update my knowledge of the family. First the sons. "So, where are Miltiades and Panayioti?"

"Canada. Toronto. They were living with my brother Michalis, but now they're big shots with jobs and have their own apartment." He spoke with equal parts admiration and disparagement.

"When was the last time they were back?"

"Two years. It's expensive, they're busy, they're *Canadians* now. They got out and they don't want to come back. I can't blame them. But not a thought they give their mother. It's more important they have their own apartment than to return to the village and cheer her up." Not a new story. Young men have been leaving the villages of Greece for the promise of the States, Canada, Australia, for many generations. Only now it's the ones with university educations. Used to be they returned to find a wife, but not so much anymore.

"And Eleni?"

"She might as well be in Canada. She's shacked up with her boyfriend in Thessaloniki. She has a job, though, a good one, with the government. Urban planning, something like that. It's what she studied at university."

"When did you last see her?"

"*Pahska*," he muttered. Easter felt like a long time ago. I hadn't seen Penelope in years. Stavros was someone I saw on the street, in the café. We didn't do a lot of house visitation. This was the first time he had visited the hut, that's how desperate he was.

"How long has Penelope been this way?"

"It started years ago, I think, but she got much worse after the boys' last visit. It's like she gave up then." He put up a hand. "I know about the empty nest thing, and sure, that must be part of it. But having a label to stick on it, that doesn't do any good. It's not like we're going to have more children! And it doesn't appear our children are going to produce any soon enough to help. And look where they live!"

We had reached the road where Stavros's truck was parked. I turned to the dogs. "Go home." They stood and stared but didn't chase the truck when we drove off. I looked up out of the window. A brilliant blue sky curved over the earth. And there was Langston, stroking and gliding above. He had no trouble keeping up with us.

Stavros had a typical stone and plaster house at the end of the village. His grandfather had built it, and except for five years in Canada as a young man, he had lived his life in it. There were a couple of outbuildings in the back. He had chickens, a few goats. His tractor was parked under a shed. There were two large olive trees in the front yard that diffused and spackled the morning sun. Two cats sat on a wall and watched. Langston fluttered to a perch in one of the trees.

The house was typically dark, and we went down a hallway to the back of the house. Off the kitchen was a room with a large fireplace, locally known as a winter room. The one window was curtained, and no lights were on. There were three chairs pulled close to the fire. Two women rose as we entered the room. Stavros introduced them. "This is Nicoletta, my sister." She must have been near my age but was already a village crone, dressed in black since their father had died ten years ago. Getting up from her chair when we entered, she had seen it was me and swiftly crossed herself. To the primitively devout, mostly women, but a few men as well, I was the anti-Christ. I needed some wild head gear or a mask that would send these believers screaming from the room. Stavros gestured toward a real old village crone, tiny, wearing a head scarf, in black, "And this is Potula, Penelope's aunt." I said, "*Yasas*." In the third chair sat Penelope, and she hadn't even turned to see who it was. Oh fuck.

Stavros walked around Penelope's chair and squatted down before her. "Look, Max has come to visit." She turned her head ever so slightly, glanced up at me, and turned back to the fire. Well, she wasn't comatose, anyway. Potula took this opportunity to get out of the house of doom, but Nicoletta didn't trust me for a second and took a stool by the door to the kitchen, where she gave me the village stare. Whatever. Stavros and I each took a chair flanking his wife. I spoke to her, but it was as though she was made of stone. It was the type of silence that sucked the sound from the room. My visiting obviously meant less than nothing to her.

Stavros stood up. "Max, I have to get to the post office before they close. I'll be back in thirty, forty minutes at the most. Is that okay? If you don't want to stay that long, just go to the café and I'll see you there."

"Oh, I can be here that long. Don't worry about it."

He thanked me and left. Nicoletta kept her vigil.

I pulled out a handful of sage from my bag and threw it on the fire. It gave the room a brief heady scent. And, I have to admit, that was about all the faux shaman had to offer. Penelope barely moved. Within that room I could feel all the prayers being said on her behalf. They hadn't helped a lick. You couldn't even burn them. The room was adorned with several icons, many Marias staring down at us, and Nicoletta was fingering a crucifix, so the Christian god had been thoroughly petitioned but hadn't granted boon. One downside of being a rationalist is you don't have recourse to prayer. Can you pray without believing in it? Holding her hand would have been inappropriate, so I spent several minutes just looking at her, trying to send a warm and friendly vibe. She had once been quite attractive but now was drawn and gray, the gray that never sees sunlight, eyes that are looking beyond this mortal coil. I had seen that look years before when my father was waiting for death to arrive. I would have liked to hear what she saw, but she kept her own counsel. There wasn't anything else to do, so I meditated. It was vaguely religious and the most present thing I could think of.

But I couldn't stay on the breath. As her silence sucked the sound from the room, so too her impenetrable solidity thickened the atmosphere. It was a darkness far blacker than you experience with closed eyes. It was the absence of everything. I tried to stay with that. After a while I found myself in an ancient palace-like building, not as a physical presence but as a floating, seeing phantom. There was a large muscled man about my age seated in a chair while an old woman washed his feet. She suddenly gasped, and then the man grabbed her by the throat and bent and whispered in her ear. What the hell, it was a scene from Homer where after twenty years Odysseus returns to Ithaka disguised as a beggar and his old nursemaid Eurýkleia recognizes him from a boar scar on his thigh. Then it went black again. What I didn't see was Penelope's namesake. Though I tried to see other parts of the building, I was only allowed this one scene before blackness wiped it out. The modern Penelope hadn't moved. And Stavros returned.

We drove back up the mountain.

"What do you think?"

I shook my head. "Stavro, like I told you, I don't know anything about this sort of thing. Nothing. I listen to people's stories but I couldn't hear Penelope's."

"What should I do?" The tone in his voice was squeezed and rough.

"Well, here's something you could do. It's sort of old-fashioned, but why don't you take her to a spa. Soak a few days in the sulfur baths, get massages, a little mud. It probably won't bring her out of depression but she'll feel better. So will you. You know, body and mind are one."

"A *spa*?" He turned from the road and gave me a

hard look. "What would *you* do if you were in the same situation?"

I had considered this while I was sitting with Penelope. "You have Canadian citizenship, don't you? I'd take her to Canada and see what they have to offer. You will probably find a wider variety of options. Your sons are there, your brother, it won't cost much, and maybe a change of scenery will help." I turned my palms up.

When I got out of the truck the dogs weren't there. I wished Stavros good luck and he drove off. Langston flew up and perched on an oak tree. "Langston, you got any insight into that level of darkness?"

He squawked.

"Yeah, that's what I thought. You should have been in that room. There are times when your bullshit just doesn't cut it. You want to help but can't, you haven't got the mojo. Or, in this case, the gri-gri. A real shaman would have engaged the evil spirit inhabiting her. You know, beat on a drum and chant for a few hours. Give her a sacred enema. I don't know. I had nothing to offer, and she wasn't interested. Being comfortable with futility, that's part of the practice. You'd think I'd have that one down by now."

He squawked.

Halfway up the path the dogs came running down, barking and eager that I pick up my pace. As the hut came into view I saw two young men, Greeks by the look of them. Whenever I left I hung a sign on my door which read: **WAIT**. Some people did. I assumed others didn't, but they left no messages so I couldn't be sure. The dogs weren't reliable witnesses, Gurdjieff didn't really give a shit about the comings and goings of humans, and Langston was a liar by nature. Jason and Dmitri were from Gythio, a port town an hour south. We loosely shared a few acquaintances. I was still undone by my encounter with Penelope and would rather have spent the day alone, but here they were.

"So what brings you guys up here?" Note I didn't offer a foot massage. I only did that with folks who had walked a long ways. These guys had the look of people who didn't walk unless they had to, though in the city that might amount to a lot. Dmitri was the talker, and also the one with the problem, such as it was. He'd spent the past few years in Athens. He'd been a student, was still classified as one, but hadn't actually attended a class in two years. Finally everyone said enough. His girlfriend hooked up with another guy, and his parents, squeezed like most by the crisis, declared they weren't going to pay his rent if he was only a pretend student. Whoa. He'd returned to his home town to consider his options.

Young Greek males are, generally, a pampered lot— and it is the work of the mothers. They hold them close and act as though they are incapable of doing anything for themselves. For instance, Greece has a national service requirement for males. Everybody able-bodied has to serve a year or so in the armed forces. One of the only ways to avoid this is to get a psychiatrist to render a report that you are too depressed to serve. As you might imagine, there's a whole bureaucratic choreography entailed in this. I've known quite a few young men who have gone this route, and in every case save one it was their mothers who were running around taking care of it: filing papers, making phone calls, arranging a session with the shrink, testifying to the judge, though in all cases these young men, adults,

were perfectly capable of doing it themselves. But why would they if mom was eager to serve? Dmitri could have been the poster boy for this whole charade.

I thought of Penelope. She had wiped those boys' noses till they'd gotten on a plane and left for Canada. In traditional Greek society they'd have married girls from the next village and brought their wives home where Mama could lord it over them, the reward for all her work. Now, though the social and economic situation was transformed, the mums were still scurrying after their lads, but without compensation.

"So what am I going to do? There aren't any jobs that pay even enough to rent an apartment, let alone eat. The university was bullshit, and I can't stand living with my parents. Now they're talking about cutting me off completely. You know, not even giving me any money!"

I couldn't stand another moment of it. I got up, made a fist, said, "Fuck this bullshit!" and thumped Dmitri a good one on the top of his head. Not enough to hurt, well, okay, maybe a little, not as violent as a slap, yet certainly enough to get his attention.

He brought his hands up in case I was going to give him another one and whined, "Wow, what did you do that for? That's not cool."

"Cool! Cool? You are so far from cool you should be burning up, but instead you're merely tepid. 'What should I do now?' What have you ever done? You're just taking up space, goddamnit! Look, I'm going to take a nap. See that pile of wood over there. It needs to be cut up into pieces this size. Use that saw. We can talk afterward." I turned, entered the hut, and closed the door.

So okay, maybe a bit of an overreaction, but sometimes you just can't bear another minute of the self-absorbed twaddle that people peddle. The bed felt great, and before I drifted off I heard the saw tearing into a log. You never know. An hour and a half later I woke to the sound of work. I glanced out the window. Dmitri was sawing away and Jason was splitting and stacking. Hot damn, sometimes a good thump is just the ticket. I made a pot of tea and stepped outside. "Hey, comrades, that is fucking great! Really, thanks a lot. That's enough. Sit down and have a cup of tea."

They came over sweating and grinning. Nothing like a little vigorous outdoor labor to get the blood flowing and settle the mind. I made some physical contact with both of them. A slap on the back, squeeze of the shoulder, often has far greater impact than stacks of words. And there are always stacks of words.

It was nearly winter, and being on the east side of the mountain, the sun set early. We sipped our tea and listened to the twilight birds.

"In a way, you are in an enviable position."

"How so? I've got absolutely nothing going on."

I stirred on my log. Dmitri flinched. "Don't worry man, I'm not gonna thump ya again. But dig it, you haven't got a care in the world. You're fed, clothed, housed, you got a little money in your pocket, you are physically fit, what the fuck, you are ready to launch but you got no destination."

Dmitri stared into his tea.

"Okay, I know. Folks my age are talking this kinda crap all the time. What I'm trying to say is that this point you're at, no responsibilities, no pressing needs, and no idea what to do next, is a wondrous place to be and may never occur in your life again."

"What do you mean?"

"Possibilities, brother! But sitting around thinking about what to do isn't going to do it. You've already done that in whatever desultory stoned-out fashion is in style these days. That's just self-fulfilling stupor. You don't want to wake up at thirty-five in the same fucking place, and maybe with a load of responsibilities that preclude you doing anything else. So it's time to start. You came up here, that means . . . well, okay, it doesn't necessarily mean that much, but it's a step. Now this might sound dumb, but just listen. You need to physically engage the world in a direct fashion. I want you to do something for someone else every day for the next month. It doesn't have to be much, but do it consciously. Don't expect to be rewarded, and try not to feel self-righteous about it. You will. But just do it. Every day. Think about it. Be aware of the needs of the world as you pass through and spontaneously respond."

"That's it? Be a boy scout or something?"

"Yeah, yeah, I know. The essence of the exercise is to break the habit of putting your own needs ahead of everything else, to break that self focus, if only for moments at a time. How does it make you feel to commit these acts? You might be surprised. You might discover skills you didn't know you had. I want you to do it for at least a month in order to introduce the idea that it could become habitual. And, one more thing, some of these acts, gestures, whatever, do them for your mother."

"My mother?"

"Yeah, her. The one who made you. Who is taking care of you to this day. That person. But, let me give you

43

a tip. Be smart about it. By that I mean, don't interfere with the order of things. So, for instance, don't try and cook lunch, though I don't imagine there's much risk of that, because that is a key element in her whole sense of being. That's what she does. But I don't think she'll have any problem with you doing the dishes. What I mean is, you are not going to change how your parents live. But you, you have the opportunity to play with the illusion of choice."

"The illusion?"

"Oh Mitso, let's leave that for later. It's getting chilly. Let's build a fire. Did you guys bring anything with you?"

Jason grabbed a small backpack and produced a loaf of bread. Dmitri pulled out of his bag a bottle of single malt. "We were told you might like some whiskey."

I clapped my hands. "You heard fucking right! Great. The bread will work. You guys build a fire in the pit here, and I'll pull together something to eat." In the hut I got out a shallow bowl, poured in a good amount of olive oil, then several cloves of garlic through a press and a generous amount of dried oregano. I had some cheese and olives, we were good to go.

Night had arrived. All creatures, save Langston, had moved toward the fire. We toasted the bread and then lapped up the garlic-enthused oil with it.

"Wow, this is really good." Jason was loosening up.

"A specialty of the house. And the whiskey goes down a bomb."

Dmitri threw some more wood on the fire. The sparks rose with the smoke. "So what did you mean about the illusion of choice?"

"Oh, you're not letting go of that one, huh?" Everybody wants the fucking secret, and nobody comes up the hill thinking they have the answer. "So, look up at that star-punctured sky. Billions of stars. Our planet is less than a fucking dot. It has no significance at all. The cosmos doesn't depend on us or this rock we're riding. Okay, that's hardly an original idea. Just like everything else, we rise and we fall, we're born and we die. And as far as I can tell, that's it. That's it. *Nada mas.* We're just part of this evolutionary genetic flow, which probably determines everything we do. We don't like this idea. Ego demands to be recognized. What about me? What about us? What about it? I don't know. As an unknown poker philosopher, homeless Jason, once said, 'The more you know, the more it sucks.' I don't agree with that, but there's plenty of truth there. By that I mean, knowing doesn't necessarily decrease suffering. Contrary to Socrates, the examined life might not have any greater value than any other. He thought knowledge and virtue were the same, truth and goodness. But it ain't necessarily so. Human happiness, for instance, isn't based on knowledge. You could probably make the argument that it's the other way around. We're temporary, my friends, just like this fire. When we stop feeding it, it goes out. And when it does . . . everything else goes on. We are an insignificant part of the going on. It's all changing. The static individual is a lie. There's this moment's pain, or pleasure, and nothing else."

"How can we live knowing that?"

"Whether we admit it or not, we've been doing it for a long, long time."

4: Comfort Daddy

While the water boiled for tea I examined my **WAIT** sign. I'd chiseled it out of a chunk of wood and strung it up with twine. I too was waiting, and while I waited, I cultivated a stillness. The stillness provided the space to speak, to pretend there was anything to say. The whole venture was driven by curiosity. I wanted to hear what was going to come out of my mouth when triggered by the questions and stories that came up the hill. I had no idea what I was doing but quite enjoyed doing it.

And the thing is, it was fascinating. Wow, the problems of the world brought to you in bite-size pieces once a week or so. I was this stranger that folks were inclined to bare their fucking souls to. It just gushed out of them. And not because I am an especially empathetic person—it was the setup that did it. That there was this guy sitting up in the mountains who would listen to your story was enough. That implied that I had empathy and would pay attention. And I did, and would pick and choose a few bits to respond to. I wasn't solving anybody's problems, if that's even possible, but I tried to propose the possibility of something else, of looking from a different angle.

They've given me one year to live."

"'Given'? I don't think that's the verb we want. There isn't anything that smacks of a gift with these predictions. It's not an addition but a subtraction."

"Whatever you want to call it. I have stage-four liver cancer. It's spread to my kidneys. I've seen the scans and the

47

rest. These people are experts, they've seen thousands of cases like mine, they have no reason to want to scare me."

"I don't suppose they do, but it is still just a prediction. Surely you've met or heard about people who were 'given' six months and are still alive ten years later. I assume you've exhausted the standard treatments?"

"All of it, surgery, radiation, chemotherapy. All of it awful, none of it worked. I'll probably die before I recover from all the treatments. I even went to Brazil and visited João de Deus, the Amazonian healer."

"You did? What was that like?"

"When you are there it feels like the most natural thing in the world. The entire scene around him promotes the idea that he has the power, that he can channel the energy of God. And he's a remarkable man with a powerful presence. And, of course, there are lots of people in the scene who claim to have been cured."

"And you?"

She shook her head. "No. I got tested upon my return and there was no improvement." She shrugged.

"But you went. I had a young friend who had cancer, and we considered going to Brazil, but in the end neither of us could summon even enough faith to seriously propose going. You are not going to take this whole trip unless you have at least some belief in this sort of healing."

"That's it, really. Someone who believed would probably say I didn't have the requisite faith, wasn't ready for a miracle. It's religious, Christian, and you might as well go to Lourdes if you believe in a god who will take a personal interest in your health."

"I can dig it. When you think about it, why would this all-loving god care how you asked for favor? Why would an all-powerful god give a shit about the level of your faith? It doesn't stand up to any scrutiny. And that's why they call it faith."

Cancer, an almost too obvious metaphor for the fate of the species: the rapidly dividing mass eating the host, the genius ability to reappear anywhere within, the reinvention and variety, it has everything going for it. But cancer doesn't strike me as the great culling cataclysm that will temper the mass, will kill toward equilibrium, unless an infectious cancer is, even now, cooking itself toward the Mayo Clinic to be born. Something will get us faster than the natural mathematical inevitability. A superplague will creep out of some tropical warren and take half of us away, or more. Perhaps it will come when much of the planet resembles the tropics, steamy and wet. Till then, we have cancer, and the condemned come seeking an herbal cure, a tincture that will purge, some magic earth sacrament administered after days of fasting, a healing vision quest, the carcinogenic antidote. Our bodies know cancer. It is so brilliantly simple. I had no hope to offer, no befeathered headdress to don in the hallucinogenic night, no progress— there is no way forward or out. I listened for the ones who were finding a certain illumination from their encounters with malignancy; it can change your head even if it isn't feeding there. There is something in the blood, the tissue, the electrical charge.

They were a bit bedraggled and weren't carrying much kit. The dogs liked them, though I didn't make too much of that. I don't believe dogs have any extra perception concerning humans. Yes, they certainly can detect fear and aggression, but they are hardly infallible when it comes to something as simple as whether a human likes dogs; having said that, I tend to take a second look if the dogs react very negatively to someone. I found Gurdjieff impossible to read. Not having much experience with donkeys, I can't say whether inscrutability is common. But there is plenty to recommend them. For one thing, they're a size you can work with. Horses, and often mules, can be intimidatingly huge. You can kinda push a donkey, whereas pushing a horse is Sisyphean. But we were talking malignancy.

Americans a long way from home, Jasmine and Melody were traveling light with a heavy load. Both lean, somewhere in their thirties, they were lifelong friends. Jasmine had stage-four cancer and a limited survival prediction. Now she and Melody were out on a global walkabout, bucket list, and vision quest. Do you make time go faster so that in one way at least you have more of it? Or do you slow down?

It was times like these I really felt the fraud. Cancer? Are you kidding me? Fatal diseases can send people out into the world ready for most anything, but what did I have to offer? Fortunately, Jasmine didn't have her hopes up for a shamanistic cure. She had quit her job, sold her house, liquidated everything, and with her lifelong friend hit the global trail. They'd been traveling now for a month and had been in Delphi before me.

"Did you get anything out of the oracle?"

"No, she was as silent as stone."

"Yeah, stone speaks to our eyes, to our hands, but never to our ears. Were you disappointed?"

She gave a short laugh. "No. I didn't expect a wild woman cloaked in fumes and herbs spouting incomprehensible gibberish to suddenly appear."

"Yeah, neither would I." I poured out the tea. "But what if she did?"

"Then I would listen very carefully."

"Bravo. Me too. The great Spanish filmmaker Luis Buñuel, scourge of the Catholic church and sometime Communist, once said, 'If the devil suddenly appeared before me, reached out a hand, and burned me with it, I wouldn't start believing. I would merely think, Ah Luis, here is yet another thing you do not understand.'"

Jasmine laughed.

"He also said, 'I'm still an atheist, thank God.' A funny guy. He sounds like he would have been great fun to hang out with, drinking cocktails and smoking cigs."

"You don't smoke cigarettes, do you?"

"No, but if I was hanging with Luis I might. Smoking appears to be an essential element, like Camus. If you were chilling with Al, not smoking wouldn't be an option."

"So your habits are situational?"

"No. This wouldn't fall within the parameters of habit, but rather knowing what the moment calls for: how to be present for the opportunity. And anyway, if you were hanging with Camus, it would be sixty years ago when cigs were good for you. And there's habits and then there's addiction."

"Situational."

"Well sure, situational it is. What else is there but the situation, this moment we're in now? The only way out of any moment is death, and we are choosing to live, if for no other reason than it sounds more interesting than the void. But that implies that we're not working with too much pain, which could tip the scales. I've been with those who can't take it any longer, and who is to argue different?"

"Where does that leave me?" she asked.

"With me. What's your pain level right now?"

She stared into the fire for a good while. "Right now I'm relaxed and there is very little pain."

"Good. Well then, we'll take a page from the Situationists, who proposed that situations be deliberately created that will facilitate directly lived experience, as opposed to the passive consumption that passes for life these days. We'll drink a little tea and then we'll take a sweat."

"The Situationists?"

"They were European social revolutionaries, a lot of them artists, who flourished in Paris from the mid-fifties to the early seventies. Check out Guy Debord's *The Society of the Spectacle*. Maybe this situation has something to do with psychogeography, though they were talking about urban environments."

Jasmine had that luminosity that can come when you are given a schedule, a program that ends. Everybody knows they're gonna die, but having the person in the white lab coat say, 'You're on the way out and it won't be long,' gets ya where ya live. It's a curse, really, knowing when, or thinking that's when. Wolves won't get you. But if you get on top of it you can see quite a ways. Of course it's the same fucking world, but your perception of it has sharpened, or that's the illusion. You live knowing, or not knowing but convinced, that the end is nigh.

Melody hardly spoke but appeared to listen quite intently. The two of them were soft and pliable. I wished I could do something, but the mountain that is cancer shaded my thoughts. Dark enters the vocabulary. Cancer can make you forget where you are. Nothing had changed. I was still a fake wise man making it up as I went along, and really, cancer shouldn't have any effect on that. It wasn't as though I could heal anyone of anything, so fuck cancer, it didn't change a thing. Nevertheless, I intended to give them the full treatment, such as it was. So first a sweat and then, the next morning, mushrooms.

I poured more water on the rocks, and they roared back with sizzle and steam. Melody sounded like she was humming, though not a tune I recognized. Then out of the dark came a truth stone, something to sharpen our wits on.

"I'll never have children now."

We let that one rise with the steam, but it couldn't get out and we were stuck with it. The sweat hut was dense with unborn steam creatures. And they were kicking.

"Did you want children?" The hot wet dark stretched out, a thick frayed spiral of swelling black.

"No, not really. Every woman considers it, or entertains the idea. It's a possibility that we know outside of mind. The situation did not occur."

"'Outside of mind.' Yeah, much of what happens is. So much of our encounter with the world is outside of mind. Most of our interaction with the world is unconscious, outside of thinking. It's called embodied cognition. It's the intelligence of the body, interacting and surviving."

"Surviving. So, what is my body doing now? Is my body stupid, then?"

Speaking in the dark resembled, curiously, talking to one's self. The other's voice felt like it was in your head, except it pushed you, demanded clarity. "Not at all. Intelligence doesn't preclude suffering or mistake, it might even guarantee it. The body is doing what it is doing, outside of mind. Your immune system is struggling, oh fuck, Jasmine, I don't know. It's fucking cancer. I haven't got a clue." Oops, the shaman façade was cracking. This was a failure I was regretting in advance.

"I don't need clues, the mystery has already been solved. It's Jasmine in the sweat lodge with the carcinogenic organs—with the tumors the size of money, or sacraments."

I kept listening.

"I don't need to know what's happening. I want to know how to live now, knowing what I know. I want to know how to live tomorrow. Death is coming toward me, what do I say? 'Hello death, what took you so long?' Only in fairy tales can you fool death. 'Jasmine? Oh, she's down the trail a ways, you can't miss her.'" She paused. "How do I live now?"

Who is talking? Who is filling the darkness with questions? These were my questions, but what were the answers? Were there any? It was like Auden's points of light. They flare up for a moment and vanish. Blink and you miss them. The irony is that they exist at all.

"What feels good?"

The three of us were fluid in the darkness, blind but smeared into each other And Jasmine answered, "This. This feels good."

We were drifting through an orchard, blessed by the sun, breathing in the smell of the earth as though we were dogs, reclaiming our animalness, our mammal bodies.

Jasmine turned and looked through me. "These memories I have, they must be a lie."

"They are."

Langston landed on a log before us. He put his head

down and paced to his left and back again. He faced us and stared. He fanned his wings out and flapped them. He did a little dance. It appeared he was gearing up for something, a pronouncement, a song, a riddle. We waited. It was easy to wait. And while we waited the current of the day flowed through us, throbbed to the ends of our appendages and past them to the rest of the world. The flux: vivid before and after, in and out of us, blurring the beginning-and-end illusion.

So why do it? Why strive to see clearly? Illusion, it would appear, is our natural condition. Though how would we know that? What does the situation require, right now? That is perhaps the only query we need. What needs to be done and how to effortlessly perform it. Or perform it with lots of effort, what the fuck.

As the butterfly flies as waves of grass swirl into tree and cliff face as being painted in an atomic improvisation. A long slow stun strokes the vicinity, inebriates the filters, breaks apart, reassembles into something with wings. Under the influence of psychotropic substances the fluidity of the world is obvious, the moisture within all living things, the humor, is the same and is flowing between. And this humor is flowing in and out of us, through the air.

Langston began to talk or squawk or whatever it is he does. He went on and on, and weirdly, bizarrely, some of what he was saying entered my ears as English. It wasn't full sentences but fragments, bursts of sense amidst the kraaack, " . . . change perspective . . . crucial . . . get above . . . if only . . . could fly . . . break off . . ." Then he flew off.

I turned to Jasmine. "Were you listening to that?"

Her eyes were profoundly dilated, her mouth was open. "He, he was talking. I could understand him. Not all of it, but he was speaking right to me and it made sense."

"What was he saying?"

"That's the strange part. Okay, all of it was strange, but while I was hearing his common crow talk, inside my head it was making sense, as though I could translate crow or something. And he was telling me I wasn't separate, that the connections would hold. And, and maybe I wasn't as much translating it as feeling it. I felt it in my soul."

"Soul?"

"Yes, soul. Don't you believe in the soul?"

"Well, tell me what you mean and I'll tell you what I think. For instance, where is it?"

"It's . . . in your heart."

"That's the standard metaphor, the cardiac explanation. Your heart is a muscle. A rather complicated one, but a muscle just the same. When they perform autopsies there has never been a report of finding some extra thing in there that you would call a soul."

"Yes, yes, of course, I know that. It's more of a spiritual essence."

"Spiritual. Do you mean in the sense of a Christian god?"

"Oh, I don't believe that whole patriarchal mythology nonsense."

"Good, neither do I. What is spirit? Is it common shared emotions? Soul, we use the term to describe music. When a musician plays in such a way that a common human emotion, sorrow, joy, is felt collectively by many, we say she plays soulfully, she has soul. In gospel music they call the hymns spirituals. Is this really much different than what we're discussing? Maybe soul means collective empathy."

"It's what connects us to everyone else. It's a spiritual

connection with the rest of the species."

"Disembodied, like the internet. So do you have an individual soul?"

"Yes, I think. But it is also part of a universal soul."

"Universal? You mean it's connected with beings on other planets?"

"Probably not. I don't know, it's the place within you that warms to affection, inspires love, compassion, it's what connects us to other humans, it's what separates us from the beasts."

I looked around at the dogs. "Are you sure?"

"Yes, or, oh, I don't know. You're supposed to know this stuff. Why are you so eager to ask me?"

"I'm fascinated by belief and why people believe what they do. Often, when I ask people, they confess that they don't know why they have and hang onto the beliefs they claim. Of course they are a cultural gift or curse, some of both, you could say. But is that all it is? Certainly we share genetic stuff with the rest of our species, and with every living thing on this planet. We are all made the same way. The same molecular setup. And yeah, when a large group of people focus on something together, it can have a powerful vibe. Political rallies, sporting events, singing in the fucking church. Collective spirit exists. We can agree on that. But that doesn't prove the existence of a soul. And why would humans have it and no other creature? Because that would mean that consciousness was involved. I think, therefore I have a soul?

"There was this Chan Buddhist monk named Chao-chou who lived during the Tang Dynasty. Chan became Zen in Japan. The Japanese owe a lot to the Chinese. But then, who doesn't owe? We are all in debt, but you can't pay with gratitude. Anyway, Chao-chou was famed for paradoxical statements and strange behavior that often led to instant enlightenment, according to legend. In the most famous story, a monk asked him if a dog had Buddha-nature, and he replied, '*Wu*'; which means, um: not, nothing, no-thing, something like that. But a basic tenet of Buddhism is that all beings have Buddha-nature. So what did he mean? There are thousands of pages written on this one encounter. It's the primary koan in Rinzai Zen. My take is that he was saying, 'There is no Buddha-nature. Let go of that idea too.' The Christian idea of the soul is similar to Buddha-nature, except I've never heard that animals have souls. A better question might be, what does it matter? Soul, no soul." I held up my palms.

"What do you mean?! Of course it does!"

"Believing in an individual soul only matters if you also believe in an afterlife, heaven, or reincarnation. Otherwise, who cares? What difference does having a soul make in how we live?"

"You're no help at all!"

"Yeah. I don't suppose I am. Is it important that there is an afterlife?"

"Of course it is. Otherwise, what would be the point?"

"Does there have to be one?"

"If there's no point why am I here?"

"I don't know. Why are you?" I realize that people found this type of exchange infuriating, but my questions were the ones I harbored. The species feels it's too important, too valuable. People wanted something I didn't have to give, meaning. What meaning? I understand that having a meaning might make it easier. "Look, if you want life after death, make art. (I almost said make a child.) As someone once sang, 'Life is short, art is long.' Sophocles is still alive on stage. But really, you decide what has meaning. It doesn't really make any difference what it is. If you decide that believing in something helps you make sense of existence, then do it. This is all we get. Either way, you die and then there is nothing. I could be wrong, but you and I will never know."

"I decide?"

"Yeah, you. Are you up to it? But 'meaning' isn't quite right, I think, in that it extends beyond you somehow. Essentially you want more pleasure and less pain. So the question becomes, what gives me pleasure. I'm not advocating hedonism here, though it works for some. What makes you feel good comes in all shapes and sizes. Maybe it's teaching small children to swim? The pursuit and use of power really turns some folks on. But on a more basic level, some type of companionship is essential for most people. It doesn't have to be a mate, but friends or a community. It could be devotion to a cause, fighting for change you believe in."

"But why would you devote yourself to a cause if life doesn't have any meaning?"

"Because it makes you feel good. And, perhaps, because you've convinced yourself that it will make a difference. Most humanist ideas are really just a mash-up of Christianity but without a nasty vengeful patriarch."

Jasmine sighed. "You're not really much of a comfort daddy, are you?"

That got me. I started laughing, and it was a minute at least before I could stop. My eyes were streaming, I could hardly breathe. The dogs were alarmed, Jasmine was laughing too. "'Comfort Daddy,' I love it! And you're right." I was still gasping. "I've never been accused of being a 'Comfort Daddy,' though I wouldn't mind. It has a nicer ring than Teiresias. I could put a sign down at the road: **COMFORT DADDY 500 meters.**"

"But you'd have to let go of all this hard-assed rationality."

"You're right, I *should* let go of that and improvise my view of life with each encounter. But I imagine I would just get back to where I am. I'm too skeptical to believe."

"But you're willing to believe your own reasoning, and where it leads."

"True that."

The mushrooms brought us together, and we stayed that way—through the night and the following days. My bed was just big enough for the three of us—we were intimate without resorting to intercourse. Mostly we kept Jasmine between us, conducting the electricity that the three of us made. She glowed.

And always the warm presence that was Melody, who listened and observed intently. Her devotion to Jasmine was intense without attachment—it wasn't important that her love be recognized, though J. did, and often. The dogs swiftly became devoted to her, sensitive to her great capacity for affection and the energy with which she realized it. We gathered wild food together.

The days meandered as though we were camped alongside the River of Time and it was a lazy stream. Down from our mountain it flowed, most of it never reaching the sea but sinking into the earth and rising up through the vegetable kingdom to the sky. It was easy. They could have stayed the rest of her life.

But one morning the current sped up and it was time to float on. Jasmine held her mug of tea with both hands and looked across the valley at the sunrise. Langston squawked, and we both looked up at him. He wasn't making any sense now, or not to me, anyway. Jasmine smiled at him and said, "Langston says it's time to go." He does? I thought that was my shtick, crow interpretation. Jasmine was becoming a real shaman right before our eyes. I should be the one leaving.

"So, Palestine."

"I know it's a bit of a cliché, but yeah, I've always wanted to go. I'll see if it speaks to me. But rest assured, I won't be hauling a cross through the streets."

"No? Pity. And after that, India?"

"That's as far as I've planned. We'll see what we find in India."

"Destination shouldn't be important. Stop and go by whim, be alert to people who raise your spirits because you are going to raise many. You are powerful right now— you are the teacher—this sentence from the doctors has illuminated you. And you know, you don't have to go. You can stay here as long as you want. Or go and come back."

"This was a good stop. Thanks for all of it. I'll remember it as long as I live." She gave me a wry smile. Gallows humor, damn, the woman is bogarting my style, helping herself to the best bits. It isn't a process of giving people things but rather of allowing them to take what they need, or want.

"I should be thanking you." I grabbed Bukowski by the ears. "In journeys such as this people often find what they're looking for."

"Really?"

"Yeah, because they define what it is they seek, and that definition is in flux."

"Oh, we're back to that," she said, "I decide what has meaning, what has value."

"And dig it. There's no evidence that I'm wrong about all this, but there isn't really anything that would prove I'm right, either. I don't care. This existence isn't a fucking game show. You don't win. Everybody loses. You can make the argument that life is not fair, but fair is a funny concept, generally applied by people who are not getting what they want. It comes to us from the English, fair play on the sporting field and all that. But if you think about it, why wouldn't someone cheat if winning was important, brought some desirable result? It's all bullshit. Life is, finally, fair. We all die, nobody gets off. So you can let go of whether it matters or not."

Jasmine threw her head back and laughed. She put a hand on my knee, squeezed, and said, "Thank you, comfort daddy. I believe I'm ready for the world."

We both laughed. Whatever I had to offer, she had received, as easy as a meal.

We didn't talk much as we walked the trail down to the road. The dogs came, and Gurdjieff carried their bags. Langston kept swooping overhead, all of us sad to see them go. It is what you discover if you allow 'meaning' to come and go. The sadness is the last reward for letting love in.

I felt like accompanying them, walking off the hill, the three of us, pilgrims bound for the Holy Land. When she couldn't walk, we would carry her, and when she lay down for the last time, we would be there. I looked around at the animals. I wasn't free. I would have to be content with the part of me she was taking away.

After a few minutes of standing by the road Panayioti drove up in his truck. A last embrace, they threw their bags into the back, climbed in the cab, and down the road they rolled, hands waving from the window. Gurdjieff let loose with a mournful bray and Langston kraawed. I knelt down, gathered the dogs to me, and wept.

5: Rave against the lying of the night

The dogs came bounding up the path yipping and howling. I could hear an acoustic guitar furiously strummed and laughter. Voices were shouting at the dogs. They were ragtag but hardly penniless, refugees from the Greek bourgeoisie, students amid the endless semester, nomads roaming the urban concrete. They were my children's peer group and gang, hedonistic comrades and victims of an uncertain truce. Now reaching their thirties, having finished with university, they were scratching out existences from the skeletal remains of the Greek economy. They had practically grown up at our house, drinking beer and smoking pot, and eating, damn could they put away the groceries.

And, happily, they still enjoyed paying a visit. They found the faux shaman routine obvious and a bit of a laugh, especially as they were very familiar with my modern house that was a mere kilometer south of the hut, but they merrily joined in. And they came bearing whiskey and drugs. And smoking—they were all vividly addicted to tobacco.

It was late afternoon, the cold was coming on, and we quickly built a fire in the pit. They wanted me to take LSD with them and trip through the night, but that sounded too ambitious. I begged off but encouraged them to self-ignite if they were so inclined. As opposed to, say, junkies, folks loaded on psychedelics can be very amusing, and I have considerable experience talking down those who find it just too exciting.

Through the night they expanded and contracted,

regrouped and scattered. The dogs were ever ready to accompany, being utterly chill with directionless wandering in the darkness.

Of all of them Melpomene was closest to my children. She had been Andromache's best friend and, briefly, the lover of Leonidas. Because my children were twins, their social circle scribed the same arc with just a few outliers claimed solely by each. She came with the usual neurotic baggage and anxiety that Greece was thoughtful enough to provide her children, but she carried it, for the most part, with a style and grace that belied her childhood as daughter of a farmer and a wool shop proprietor. She lived in Athens and was involved in all aspects of the performing arts: actor, writer/director, stage and costume design, choreography, promotion, video, whatever. And, naturally, she waited tables at a hip café—the traditional life of a young person attempting to work in the arts. She often had wonderful tales of her life in the theatre world. And, a bonus, she often had her latest beau in tow. She had excellent taste in companions, but today she was just part of the gang.

"How's Maki doing?" It was always her first question, even though she was well aware of what Andromache was doing via Skype and social media. But I might know something different.

"She's thinking of moving to Brooklyn, which is a bit of a cliché, I would think."

Melpomene nodded with a grin. "Brooklyn, yeah, I know about that. She keeps bugging me to move to New York, but I haven't got the money together. There's always something that requires what little funds I have."

"Deciding to work in the theatre is like taking a vow of poverty."

"Tell me about it. Fact is, Maki's proposed move to Brooklyn is partly about me. There isn't enough room for me where she lives now."

"That's for sure. Glorified closet is an exaggeration. It works because she has the studio, where she spends most of her waking hours. She just sleeps there. I don't think she cooks much."

Melpomene laughed. "No, I'm sure she doesn't."

"So, Mene, what's the scene in Athens like these days?"

"Active. New groups appear every month, it seems, and new spaces for performance. Nobody is making any money, of course, but the scene is vital with room for all kinds of theatre, guerrilla street to drawing room. There's room for more improv. And video production is much the same. I'm looking to do more comedy. I'm tired of directing. It is such a screaming hassle trying to corral a group of egomaniacs, which near all actors are. I want to be the maniac for a while."

"Do you think you could get work in New York?"

"Everybody wants to think they could. As an actress, maybe. It would take years before I could do there what I do here, especially directing. Maybe never."

"New York is full of ambitious talented people from somewhere else."

"That part would be fun. To work with that kind of expertise and ambition is great. I'm not intimidated by that. It's just that I think Athens is on the cusp of things. The chaos of the age is more advanced here. We have the crisis and the flood of immigrants and refugees. The mix of Asia and Europe. Old Greece is collapsing, and we have to figure out how to make it new. This society is more dynamic than it has ever been. There's a lot of energy, and I want to be part of that action: theatre and video, media, has a large role to play. We have to frame the questions."

"What is the question?"

"Same as it ever was. How do we create sustainable communities? How do we empower indigenous leadership? How do we live now, while careening from crisis to crisis in the amusement park of late capitalism? Iphigenia can give you more concise questions than I can. I'm opting for creative action over the chance of success."

We gave that a long hard consideration. "But you know, this only applies to what I want to do. For others, leaving makes sense. For instance, Odysseus wants to make contemporary music, all kinds. He needs to go to America. He's dying to go. And he will when he gets it together. Soon, I think."

Paris was the most beautiful and the most frustrating of them, tall and lean, with a cascade of light brown curly hair and a dreamy, sleepy demeanor that young women couldn't get enough of. It wasn't an act, he was sleepy and lazy and utterly lacking in ambition. And yet, as I said, he was extremely lovable, without enemies and welcome wherever he went. My son had said his most admirable quality was his complete lack of ambition.

A crashing in the dark, vegetation breaking, force being randomly applied, a snort, or was that a grunt. Paris winced and rose to his feet, ready for flight. "What was that?"

I knew who it was, but cocked my head and listened for a moment to the crashing in the underbrush, stretching out the mystery, letting a bit of danger waft in. "That's Seesmós, he's the alpha boar on this mountain."

"What, you have a pet boar named Earthquake now?"

"Pet? Oh no, Seesmós is nobody's pet. He's a fucking wild boar, and he's sired many swine in these parts. You see," I tilted my head back and looked down my nose, "he's in his prime." I didn't get even a grin. Referencing Miss Brodie to non-native English speakers born in the late '80s, what an exercise in futility. "Someday a younger, tougher boar will come along and drive him off the mountain, but that pig hasn't shown up yet."

The dogs were used to Seesmós. During their first encounters they had gone nuts, barking hysterically and making little feints toward the boar, but Seesmós was too quick, they couldn't get close enough for even a wee nip. And they fully realized that if he got hold of one of them, it would be deep shit. I suppose if they had coordinated their attack they might have done some damage, but their unity only applied to making noise. They were worthless in the hunt, but on this mountain we were hunting illusion, not game. For that venture they acted as a Greek chorus, barking their incoherent commentary and warning of greater illusions looming in the night.

"Are we safe?"

I laughed. "Safe? From what?"

"From Seesmós! Will he attack?"

"Seesmós? *Seegah*. Last I heard, human flesh wasn't part of his diet. If you encounter a sow with piglets, she might be aggressive, but that's not likely. The only dangerous thing in these woods is man. I'd venture to guess that you are the most dangerous creature in the night."

"Me?"

"Yeah. You are more likely to hurt yourself than anything else out there."

"What do you mean by that?"

"Besides the fact that you're loaded? Well, your separation from your environment, your inability to commit to anything, your unresolved relationship with your parents . . . need I go on?"

"What? You mean everything is my fault?"

"Fuck fault. But even though you have no control over your life, you have to own it. Pretend that you are responsible, that your decisions matter. Pretending to be something is all we do, whether you believe it or not. That's what I'm doing."

"Even if you're right, what good would that do?"

"It allows you to act." I threw a log on the fire. See*smos* had moved on. "Belief can make experience more intense, as though you have more at risk." I looked around at my canines. "More dogs in the fight, if you will. The paradox is that while you have no control over existence, you create the world you experience."

"What the hell does that mean?"

"It means, if you think piloting a bus through the urban chaos is a revolutionary act, it is. When Dylan sang, 'It may be the devil or it may be the lord, but you gotta serve somebody,' he was talking about finding something to believe in, something more important than you. Something to put yourself in service to."

Paris stared into the fire, his olive skin glowed. He had a look of fierce concentration and turned to me. "Well, what are you serving?"

"You right now, I suppose. And while I do that, I'm also trying to see whether the knots I tie myself into can be undone using a different path, in a thinking-out-loud sort of way."

"I don't get it."

"That's cool. Someday you'll realize just how full of shit I am, but until then . . ." I turned my palms to the dark above us, then clapped them. "So what's it gonna be, Paris? What wagon are you gonna hitch yourself to?"

We watched the smoke and sparks rise. An owl hooted nearby. I couldn't see Langston. He must have retired for the evening. But I hadn't.

"Or not. Consider Seesmós the symbol of your fear. Fear is not necessarily a bad thing. It was crucial for the survival of the species. Maybe it's crucial for your survival? What's interesting to consider is, does the fear hold you back from interesting and/or pleasurable experiences, rather than just keep you alive. That's something to consider."

"I don't need my life to be more interesting."

That stopped me, bang. What bullshit I was talking. Commit to something, put yourself in service to what? Fear? Why not a nice easy life that he already knew how to live? A life where nothing was expected of him. He had a wide circle of friends, never lacked for female companionship, and could always find a gig. He was doing it. The whole discussion was my projection, my vanity and desire speaking. A nice mellow small town life wasn't enough, no, you had to strike out for the territories or wherever the adventure of the new glowed. What cliché-ridden crap. I bowed to Paris and his indolent sensuality. Why not? "Paris, you're right. You have found your place without looking. Bravo. We should all be so lucky."

Paris shrugged.

They all wandered through the night. A generation ago they might be married with children, but now, thirty years old, they career through the night loaded on acid wondering what's next. From the static to the dynamic, and yet, what is more dynamic than producing human life?

"And I think my spaceship knows which way to go."

Odysseus was a bouncing, high-energy kind of guy. He only sat down when he was playing guitar, which was often. If he was talking he was walking, in circles if need be. He too seemed tall to me. This generation of Greeks, having sat down to a middle-class diet every day, was much larger than the previous, which made most of them, the males at least, taller than me. He and my son Leo had studied music together, but whereas my son swiftly reached a level of proficiency on his instruments and then lost interest, Odysseus burned to play.

"Mene says you're itching to get to the States."

"Definitely, dude. I nearly got the money together."

"Great. Where?"

Odysseus gave me a long look. "Where do you think?"

Of course, why did I ask? I started whistling the opening bars of "New York, New York."

"That's what I'm talking about. I got a place to crash, enough money for, eh, if I don't pay rent, a year."

"Really? Congratulations. I applaud your determination. You are so ready, man. You'll tear 'em up."

"That's the plan." He hit a chord. "Hey, man, you got your sax here?"

"Of course, it's in the hut. As a friend recently put it, I come from the Anglo-saxophone world."

Odysseus, head bobbing, body swaying, started rolling

out a churning jagged rhythm on his guitar and gave me his irresistible grin. "Then what are you waiting for? Let's jam."

I dusted off my horn. I only play when there are people to play with. Playing by myself, practicing, has no appeal, but Odysseus and I had played together for many years and always raised a joyous noise. I brought out a couple of hand drums and a penny whistle in case anyone wanted to join in. We started at a terrific pace but soon slowed to a spacy blues-type thing. I followed Odysseus. Soon enough Iphigenia came out of the dark and took up a drum. Stein and Bukowski joined in with howls and moans. Gurdjieff moved closer and threatened to bray. We wove a fractured fantasy through the olives and pine, the oak and chaparral. The odd owl punctuated our sonic reveries with hooing grace notes. Then Melpomene appeared to coax a certain tonal madness from the dogs. She stood before them like a choir master and got them all emoting a low plaintive *ooooiiiiiiii*. And the creatures of the Tayegetos moved closer to our flame, the dogs giving us animal kingdom credibility in the Lakonian night.

"This is ground control to Major Tom"

Iphigenia's hair was always casually knotted in such a fashion that half of it was sticking out, hanging down, something to push away, but never the same way. It was the quintessential don't-give-a-fuck look which, done with the proper élan, seemed the height of style, or anti-style. Though they all aggressively resided on the far left of the body politic and had spent years demonstrating and rioting in the streets of Athens, Iphigenia was the most dedicated. She had taken a degree in political science and was ever expanding her grasp of the theoretical concepts. Her dialectic was razor sharp, her devotion to the cause of human liberation seemingly indefatigable. She was a physical wreck: emaciated, fatigued, wracked by nail-biting, chain-smoking tension. The revolution is very stressful. Despite all that, she looked years younger than her twenty-nine, with wet, poignant eyes and a voice soft, almost a whisper.

She was living in a squat in Athens occupied by Syrian refugees and provided organizational strategies, community liaison, fund-raising, Greek lessons, and whatever else was needed. She had swiftly gained a rudimentary grasp of Arabic, and this enabled her to at least partially integrate into the community.

"Empowerment is what it is all about. I help locate the wagon, they fill it and pull it where they want it to go. What these people have seen, my god, we know nothing. It is far more horrible than you can imagine. Slaughter, rape, twenty-four-hour-a-day misery, continual betrayal, small children on their own. But some become energized, more vital, and they in turn pull others along. What we have at the squat is a shattered working class who sold everything they had in order to get out. There is nothing to go back to. When the crazies with guns start getting close, could be government, could be ISIS, you get out however you can. You pay the man whatever he asks. We can't think in terms of progress. Do we have enough food? Do we have water? Can we keep warm? How do we enforce the bare minimum of rules decided on? Movement is barely discernible and then swift and brilliant. It's not about victories. Oh fuck, who is cleaning the goddamn toilets? It's about getting up in the morning and doing it again. The same damn thing.

You know, Mene does children's theatre at the squat once a week. She's just great with the kids."

"Really? She didn't mention it when we were talking earlier."

"Well, you have to remember, we're on acid."

"Best not to forget. How's that working for you?"

She drifted off and stared at the illuminated trees. I took a pull of whiskey and stoked the fire.

She slowly rotated her head toward me and said, while gesturing toward the fire with both hands, "We have to develop new techniques. These communities, not only are they full of traumatized people, babies to *yiayias*, but they are extremely transitory. They're not staying. Most of them want to move on into rich Europe. They're waiting for papers, or word from relatives in Germany or France. For something, they want to move on. So a large part of our efforts is spent securing the basics: shelter, water, food, heat in the winter. How do you organize a community when the majority of possible members, not citizens, intend to leave?"

"I guess you try to teach survival techniques and ways of seeing."

Iphigenia gave me her most endearing smile. "It's good to talk to you again, my friend. We get so wound up in the city, racing from crisis to trauma to accident. I guess you'd say everything is an accident."

"Including us. But how are you doing? You look frazzled and underfed."

She sighed and lit another cig. "Yeah, that about sums it up, 'frazzled and underfed.' I eat at the squat, of course, but when I'm there my mind is racing with the next ten tasks. I can't just relax and eat. There are several women there trying to be my mother." She laughed. "Fuck, I have enough mother already. We came down to have a little holiday, but if I'm at my parents' house, every conversation degenerates into two subjects. Why am I not moving toward marriage, hell, why don't I have a steady boy, and why would a university graduate choose to live like a refugee?" She exhaled a lungful of smoke. "Right now I have my phone turned off. I know it's making her furious. And I refuse to check how many text messages she's left."

I nodded, grabbed a ball of smoke from the fire, and blew it into a hawk that became a Buddha and then a self-immolating monk. Nobody ever asks the poor if they want a war.

> *"And I'm floating in a most peculiar way*
> *and the stars look very different today."*

Odysseus wandered in with Bukowski and Stein. "Hey, have you guys sorted out the world yet?"

"We're discussing the current miseries."

"Which episode?"

"Miseries, not mini-series, *pethi mou*. Though one's probably in development. What would we call it?"

"Everything is infamy."

"Maybe we could steal stories from Borges?"

"Rhizome," said Iphigenia.

Heads perked up. "Now we're talking. That title would facilitate a series of independent yet connected stories."

"Underground and overground, brother."

"What's this? What are you guys talking about?" Melpomene's performance radar was finely tuned to any possible opportunity to occupy space with body and voice. She arrived with Voltaire and sat down by the fire.

"We're proposing a mini-series called 'Rhizome,' I believe."

She nodded. "What's the premise?" We collectively considered this, with great concentration. Our group throbbed.

I thought it was up to me to get the ball rolling, so I threw out one of my favorite story lines, the itinerant players. "Okay. We have a traveling theatre group who are wandering the islands during the summer putting on plays at refugee camps."

Melpomene jumped right in. "Would they be existing plays or improvised or collectively composed?"

"A mix. Remember, we're working with hour-long episodes. You're not going to show the entire play, obviously. 'Waiting for Godot' is an obvious, maybe too obvious choice."

"But what's their real motive? They can't just be staging plays. There should be some type of covert political activity."

"Maybe they're providing false documents that allow the refugees to get off the island, to move further into Europe?"

"Maybe they have a boat."

"A boat?"

"They're selling drugs."

"They have a magic drug that allows people to teleport."

"And they're trying to find those that are ready. Not worthy, note."

"Whether or not they have some political activity besides the plays they stage, the setup would provide lots of opportunities to tell stories. You have the evolving ones within the troupe, and you have all these refugee stories.

Each episode could be on a different island at a different camp."

"Oh, better yet," Melpomene was amping up, "each episode is at least partially improvised at the refugee camps with their input. Obviously, refugees will be playing the refugee parts. It can be a collective production. A collective production that reveals yet another aspect of the refugee situation."

Iphigenia gave Melpomene a high-five.

"You would need to form a collective theatre troupe that also has technical skills in video production."

"Each episode could be directed by a different member of the group."

"You'd do the same with camera and sound, so that while there was a unity to the whole series, each episode would reflect a different perspective."

"And the theatre troupe would continually encounter, at each camp, some sort of Syrian mafia who would make things difficult."

We all fell silent, pregnant—with drug-enthused possibility.

"Take your protein pills and put your helmet on."

Time unspooled.

Paris, speaking to no one, to all, "Let's burn some meat on the grill."

"Um, we don't have any meat."

"Fuck the meat, let's burn our brains on the grill!"

A sound idea. "I suggest, rather than oregano we use Agamben."

"O, torture me with theory!"

"Sure. 'The Camp as the Nomos of the Modern. The

camp is the space that is opened when the state of exception begins to become the rule.'"

We all turned to Iphigenia. "The camps are not only depriving these people of citizenship but, ah," she snapped her fingers, "what's the word, agency over their lives."

Paris asked, "What's that mean?"

Odysseus came back with, "A is not Z. Blood is not water. Oxygen is not atmosphere. But death, death is the end."

"Whatever."

Iphigenia circled round on that. "That's true. Agamben proposes a concept he calls 'whatever singularity.' It's like a rejection of the conditions of belonging or identity and how this threatens the state."

"'Whatever singularity'?"

"Yeah, crazy, huh, but what he means by 'whatever' is being that always matters, no matter what. So that while we use 'whatever' to indicate a certain blasé attitude, lack of concern toward the situation at hand, he uses it to mean being able to act whatever comes down the road."

"Well slap my face."

"We define things not only for the sake of convenience but as a means of control. Do we allow the state to define us?"

"Okay, who are we?"

"What."

"What?"

"*What* are we? That is the question."

"We are a throbbing orb in the Lakonian night that will grow legs by morning."

Dawn is the answer for the question of night. I awoke before sunrise, boiled water, and tossed some wood on the still glowing embers. Only Stein was waiting for me. Langston was back on his perch. "Yo crow, where is everybody?" He scrawked and flew off. The sun came on in flashes of orange and rose, rays of it sheared the morning mist into geometric planes that hovered over the valley.

Odysseus loped in accompanied by Bukowski. He had a dreamy look and merely nodded while he accepted tea. The clomp of hooves announced Gurdjieff's arrival with a beaming Paris on his back. We don't know the name of the donkey Jesus rode into Jerusalem, but he couldn't have looked more beautiful than Paris on Gurdjieff at sunrise. A man on a horse commands, but on a donkey invites. He slid off his mount and held his hands out to the fire. "What a great animal Gurdjieff is. Do you have like a brush or something? You know, to kind of groom him?"

"Yeah. It's right over there by the door of the shed. He loves to be brushed."

Then laughter came up the trail. Accompanied by Voltaire, Derrida, and O'Keeffe, Iphigenia and Melpomene walked in, arms around each other and laughing from their diaphragms. Big bucket pratfall laughs that rolled over us like the sea, like a brilliant healing elixir.

They broke into dawn like they were the first on the planet and I was the last of the previous species who had been waiting for their arrival with fire and tea. We collectively caressed the dawn, all of us touching something, a tree, a dog, a donkey, each other.

6: The conditions of love

"You can also look upon our life as an episode unprofitably disturbing the blessed calm of nothingness." −Schopenhauer

Nobody seeks a second opinion if they like the first. Up on the hill here I amount to the fourth or fifth, I believe. Sometimes I'm part of the endgame, the unwinding of the philosophical spool, the shedding of belief and doubt. Anger is something that turns the spool, that wraps the fury tighter. Release is a vital element. Release, it holds a spectrum of meaning. We catch and release. In biological terms, at least, a man releases and a woman receives, any day now I shall be, to make available—for public consumption? A discharge. Remit.

I'll tell you, my childhood doesn't interest me much. I rarely think of it. I can't remember any traumatic events that pointed inexorably toward . . . what? I don't feel like I'm carrying anything, some weight that is holding me back, something that jerked me around and made the next part of my life inevitable. What would that be? It sometimes feels that people hang onto their childhood as an essential part of their personality. But the hanging smacks of longing. And what the fuck good is that?

Rather than childhood trauma, what I was given to struggle with was a resistance to belonging. I was always resisting assimilation into the group, the organization, the class. I didn't have any difficulty with friendship, would gladly participate in the team, but only if it was anarchic or if I was the leader. Put a coach in the equation and I was out of there, either voluntarily or through authoritarian ostracism. Same in the classroom. Certainly the desire to receive the attention of others played into this, the guy who was talking, joking, getting thrown out. Reprimanded. Reprimanded. The banal solutions for coercion. The demands to, if not obey, to blend in, bend, placate, submit. I couldn't have worked for the government, as part of that vast organization. Not for any significant amount of time. And the army, I can't imagine. I would have been on permanent latrine duty. I'd have lived in wellies.

When you break it down, it's obvious I couldn't have worked for any company or party. Same with country. I did not want to belong. I wonder why I am like this? I don't in any way advocate this approach as something admirable, as a path to the good life. Just is. What is the mathematics of any of us, infinitesimal germs amidst chaos vast beyond comprehension? My parents were independent sorts but had no trouble joining and belonging. I don't think I can blame them, but maybe that means I'm just not looking deep enough? My children, on the other hand, having been moved to Greece at a young age, exhibit a marked fluidity and ease at joining and belonging. Regardless of who or what gets credit, biology or atmosphere, this trait has led inexorably to this hut in the mountains with the animals, where the only thing I belong to is the planet.

It was a warm, beautiful afternoon on the mountain. Down in the valley it was scorching. You could see the heat rising, bending the air, hallucinating the orchards and the mountains to the east. Sparti is often the hottest place in Greece, with temperatures in the low to mid forties.

As I said, it was just right on the mountain. Everything was napping, birds, dogs, and I was dreaming away in a hammock. Suddenly we were all snapped out of our reveries by a firmly voiced and unmistakably American "Hello, is anybody here?"

The beasts, who in this heat were crap watchdogs, roused themselves and let out a few perfunctory barks. I struggled and flailed about in my hammock, discombobulated by this abrupt return from the land of nod, summoned by an America I kept at a long arm's length. I looked over the edge of the hammock, and there before the hut were two glowing examples of the American bourgeois dream life, like adverts for milk or toothpaste, shampoo. America at its best always looks like it is selling something. They were blonde, bronzed from the sun, brilliant teeth, fit and athletic, smartly decked out, a cliché, really. I managed to swing my feet out of the hammock and answered, "Yeah, yeah, someone is here. We'll figure out who in a moment."

They dropped their backpacks and got acquainted with the dogs in a relaxed and easy way. I dropped to my feet and pushed myself erect. I shook my head, damn, I could have gone on for another hour, easy. We did the intros.

May and Richard, in their early thirties, siblings from Minneapolis holidaying in Greece, what need had they of a faux shaman Oh how we love the surface of things, we don't even have to use our imaginations. We can just glide across the surface like a frozen lake or a television program. There's no investment required.

"How did you get here? I mean, what led you here? I don't think I appear in guidebooks or anything. I certainly hope not."

"We were at the beach." May pushed her hair aside.

"Near Gythio. Vathi, it's called. Kronos Camping, that's the name."

"I know it well. Actually, I'm often down at the beach near there. I could just as easily not be here. Some sort of luck involved, I'll let you decide what kind."

May tilted her head and looked at me. "We met a guy at the café there who said we should visit you before we returned to the States. I'm not sure why."

I laughed. "That's often what people ask themselves *after* visiting me. What was this person's name?"

"Mitso. He's about your age."

"Aha! You met Shrink Dogg!"

"Shrink dog?"

"Yeah. He's a psychiatrist. Shrink Dogg is his rap handle. That's with two Gs, like Snoop. Sometimes he takes a boom box with his beats on it and walks the beach rapping. The kicker is that he riffs off stuff he hears in therapy sessions, with a layer of anonymity, of course. It's delightfully weird shit."

"Oh. We didn't hear any of that."

"Pity. It's in Greek, of course."

Whew, it's a lot more comfortable up here than it is down there." Richard was gym-muscled and confident, in a tank top and shorts, stretching, revealing his delineation and his bemusement with the whole thing.

"Yeah, Sparti's a fucking oven." We were all taking a long drink of water. "So what brings you guys up here?"

"Well, we're heading back to Athens, and you're on the way. Your friend in Vathi, Shrink Dogg, I guess, really sold you as an attraction."

I laughed. "An attraction. Finally I've become a

destination! That's great, though, that you aren't seeking advice or something. Most people are, but I enjoy guests. Everyone who comes up here has something to say. And, generally, the next day, they leave." I looked at them wondering what Mitso saw and assumed I would find out soon enough.

Richard pulled two six-packs of half-liter cans of Heineken out of a plastic bag, still cold and beaded with sweat. "We did bring some beer, though."

"Richard, not Dick?"

"Never."

"Cool. Richard, thanks for shagging the brew. As I don't have any chill capacity, we'd better start drinking it now."

"Suits me." Richard handed us each a beer and we punched tabs.

"To joy." We touched cans and drank.

"Wait a second." I held up my hand. "I have chairs!"

May and Richard gave a puzzled look as I unfolded three deck chairs a friend had found in a dumpster in Sparti.

"They may not look like much, but they are luxury compared to sitting on those rounds of wood there." They looked, turned back, plopped themselves in the chairs, and settled in.

Eventually that icy surface you're skating on thins and begins to crack. What you see is not enough, and the underneath struggles up and demands attention. Insists. Richard and May's lawyer father had moved out of the house when they were in their mid-teens and gone to Florida with a new, younger woman. He now taught in a junior college in Sarasota and spent a lot of time on the beach. They were pointedly brief about it.

May was a big woman but not bulky. Her tank top revealed the arms and shoulders of a swimmer. "How did you find the sea in Vathi?"

"Oh, it was great. Warm, clean, I swam at least an hour every day. I swim back home and in the summer in the lakes. You know, land of ten thousand lakes? But it's way different in the Aegean. You're really buoyant. 'Cause the salt content is so high, I guess. It takes less effort and you go faster. I loved it." They attracted the attention of the dogs, who came to them without any coaxing. Voltaire was resting his head on her feet.

"Do you have dogs?"

"Not now. I'm in an apartment, which I can't possibly keep. I'll have to start thinking about moving when I get back. That so sucks. But my mom, she has dogs, and we had them growing up. I'd love to have a place big enough to have a dog. But I probably won't."

"Your mom, she's still in Minneapolis?"

"Oh yeah. She's in real estate. But, believe it or not, she's in Alaska right now fishing with her new guy. They get flown in to some remote lake and catch trout or something." She shrugged. "I like it here, thank you."

"What's your job?"

"I'm a legal aide. I should have gone to law school but I'm too lazy to do all that studying. The firm I work for does a lot of personal injury claims, that kinda stuff."

"Do you and Richard often travel together?" Her brother had taken up residence in the hammock.

May prefaced any statement by pushing a long flaxen lock out of the way, hooking it behind a reluctant ear. "No, but Richard was nice enough to accompany me on this trip. I'm in recovery from a really shitty breakup."

"Relationship crash. I hear a lot of that up here."

May gave me a quick annoyed look. Nobody wants their troubles shoved together with everyone else's, not by a fucking stranger, anyway.

I tried to ease her concerns. "It's the pressure of the age. The consumer society raises everyone's expectations and consequently they're often disappointed." I shrugged, "That's one reason, anyway." Just one item off an extensive menu.

"I was with Rob for three years. He was so romantic. He took me to the coolest places, shows, restaurants and stuff. We went to Hawaii one winter. We were really in love, living together in a really nice apartment. We made lots of plans. We were going to get married and have kids and everything! We'd even started looking at houses. Even my mom liked him."

So far so banal, though when real estate starts to get involved, things are turning serious. "What else did Rob do besides the feet-sweep thing?"

"Huh? Oh, yeah. Ha ha. He's a lawyer specializing in internet law, so he's at the capitol a lot. Some of what he does you'd probably call lobbying, you know, trying to get laws written that help his clients."

"Sounds like lobbying to me."

"Yeah, it does. He made pretty good money at it. You know, drove a beamer and had nice stuff, but he wasn't an asshole about it or anything. He volunteered two nights a month at the Legal Aid clinic."

"A secular saint."

May gave me an angry look. "Wow, you're cynical."

The impulse to choose sides, while often correct and

viable in politics, is often counterproductive on a personal level. "You're right. My bad. He was a great successful guy; probably good-looking too."

May looked down toward the valley and rubbed her nose with the back of her hand. "Yeah, he was."

"And then it went south."

May emitted a dramatic groan. "Literally."

"What, he moved to Florida too?"

She gave me an odd look, and I felt like I had overplayed my hand. Maybe it wasn't all daddy abandonment, though that certainly felt like the territory.

"He went to a convention in Las Vegas, technology law, something like that. And after a few days he emailed me, emailed me! That it was all over and he was moving to Los Angeles. Not even a fucking phone call."

"The swine." Maybe it's just a matter of knowing your moment.

"No shit, it fucking sucks. He's getting his stuff out of our apartment while we're in Greece. I couldn't bear to see him. What a coward! A fucking email! Didn't want to try and explain himself over the phone, let alone in person. I get it, nobody wants to play the jerk, but sometimes you have to take responsibility. Our years together meant nothing to him, I guess." May crushed the beer can in her hand. "This from the man who claimed over and over again that he loved me unconditionally."

"Theoretically one could love someone unconditionally and still fall in love with someone else, I suppose. But really, 'unconditional love' is the Easter Bunny of pop culture, especially in America. You don't hear it mentioned in Europe. Don't get me wrong here, but my experience is that the only people who bring up this idea are folks who want to receive it but aren't. I've never met anyone who wanted to love someone unconditionally but couldn't. Though I know it occurs. Sometimes parents just can't get into the children they have conceived and are trying to provide for. We are not all on the same fucking program! The only things we are guaranteed to share with every other living thing on the planet are suffering and death."

"The Easter Bunny?"

I shrugged. "Yeah. Think about it. Unconditional love is in the realm of religion. That's something a god would or could do. It's not something humans are capable of. It's too big, too vast. All human relationships are a process of negotiation, except for infancy, where the mother's feelings may resemble something akin to the unconditional, but once that child becomes a social creature, no. You want it because you don't want to be responsible. Whatever you do you'll be loved. You act like a brat, you'll be loved. You steal a car and get arrested and thrown in jail and daddy has to come down to bail you out, you'll be loved. You utterly reject daddy because he's trying to deny you something that you want, and you'll be loved. Or better yet, you kill your brother. Is daddy still going to love you? It begins to sound dumb after a while. It is not how we function."

"Wow, that's harsh. But in my case, I know my daddy didn't love me at all."

"Or, at least, he loved something else more."

"No, it was less than that. He never looked back. He didn't give a shit about us, and after all these years, he sure as hell ain't coming back."

"Nor is his surrogate."

"Amen to that." She popped another beer and rubbed Stein behind the ears.

Gurdjieff lazily moved nearer. The animals didn't enjoy the heat, whereas I rather liked it. May stood up and stroked the donkey. "Wow, It's cool you have a donkey. Do you ride him?"

"Sometimes, especially when we're fetching water. He can carry quite load."

"So, his name, Gurdjieff? Was he someone famous, from the past or something?"

"He was an Armenian Greek mystic spiritual teacher and con man in the first half of the twentieth century. He was very well travelled and had followers all over the place. He's fun to read. Check out a book called *Meetings with Remarkable Men.*"

May retrieved a notebook from her pack and jotted this down. It was too hot and dry for a fire, no matter how socially cohesive they are, and I had a few lamps lit to cut the darkness. We were in that twilight transition when the roar of the cicadas calms down and the crickets take over, and for a while both are in an entwined murmur, a susurrus if you want to be poetic, until finally it's all crickets save one lone cicada getting in his last clacks. The dogs, after being rousted by the excitement of visitors, were snoozing away.

D o you live up here like all the time?"
"Most of the time. I have other places I can be."
A stroke of the luck, that.

"So this setup here, with the hut and everything, it's not the complete picture, is it?" May was curious.

"The complete picture? No, but then, what possibly could be? I'm not finished yet. and neither is the world. When do you return to Minneapolis?"

"We fly out of Athens in three days. I wish we had a couple more weeks. I'd go right back to the beach and start swimming."

"Instead?"

"I'm back to work. We arrive home on Saturday, and Monday morning I'm working. And I've got to start looking for a new place, pack, move. The whole thing totally sucks."

"The world conspiring against you."

"Sure feels like it sometimes."

"I have a suggestion. An exercise, if you will."

"Yeah?"

"Try going through the day taking nothing personally. This is the truth of reality, none of it is about you. Someone gives you grief, they're having a bad day, let it pass. Rob leaving you is about how he feels about his life and the people he's around. You are not the cause of any of that. The billions of bits of phenomena floating, twinkling in his wake, the fireflies of what was, they're the cause."

"Huh?"

"You know how when you're in a bad mood everything pisses you off, feels like it is personally fucking with you: the weather, the traffic, the line at the supermarket, things breaking or malfunctioning, people not calling you when you expected. Depends on just how bad your day is."

"Sure, everybody does that."

"Reverse that. No matter what happens, it is just the world floating by. You acknowledge it and move on, let it pass, because you are taking nothing personally, including acts that are aimed right at you. For instance, your mother gives you grief over the phone. It's just your mother acting out her own fears and problems. It's not about you, it's about her. Don't empower the world. Slow the pace of your reactions down. Take a breath before you do anything, and remember, it's not about you."

We rested in the ringing hum of crickets. "May, let me tell you a little Zen story that touches on what I was saying. It's medieval Japan, and on the outskirts of a small town lives Hakuin, a monk renowned for the purity of his life and practice. Near Hakuin's hut live a couple who run a small shop. They have a teenage daughter. One day they discover she's pregnant. Oh shame and disgrace! The young woman doesn't want to get the father in trouble so she fingers Hakuin. The couple race over to Hakuin and give him big grief. His response is, 'Is that so?' When the child is born, the parents take it to Hakuin and say, 'Here, you produced this child so you take care of it.' Hakuin, his reputation ruined, accepts and takes care of the baby, getting milk from neighbors and giving the infant all it needs. After a year the young mother can't stand it any longer and confesses that the father is a young man who works in the fish market. Argh, the parents go back out to Hakuin confessing their shame and raining apologies down on him and take the child back, to which Hakuin merely says, 'Is that so?'"

May laughed. "Good story. So you're saying, deal with what you can and don't worry about what you can't control. Good luck, bad luck, it's all the same. Easier said than done, I would think."

"Ah, so."

What did you do when you finished high school, Richard?"

"I enlisted in the Marines."

"The Marines. And they sent you where?"

"Iraq."

"How exciting."

Richard gave me a hard look.

"Excuse me. Why? Why did you join the Marines?"

"I wanted to serve my country." It felt like he was about to add a 'sir' to every statement, either at the end or the beginning.

"Does your family have a military background? Your father, for instance?"

"He didn't serve. But my uncle Dave did. Two tours in 'Nam."

"Are you close to your uncle?"

"Yes (*sir*), I am. He picked up the slack when my father left. He's the one who came to the games, took us to the lake. Did all the dad stuff."

"Was he in the Marines?"

"Ye*s (sir),* second lieutenant. He was in ROTC at college."

"Did he used to talk about his experiences in Vietnam?"

"He still does sometimes. We talk about what happened, in my war and his."

"How did he feel about your enlisting?"

"We talked about it a lot. We knew I'd probably see some fighting, and he wanted to make sure I knew what that meant."

"What does it mean?"

Richard stared off to the east. "It tests your commitment and requires total focus. Bonding with your unit is crucial. But before all that is the training you received, and in the Marines you are prepared to fight. *(Sir.)*"

"I got that part. But what does combat mean? To you."

"It tests you and whether you have courage. I used to think it was part of becoming a man, facing combat." Pause. "I don't think that anymore."

"What caused this change of mind?"

"After I left the service I went to the University of Minnesota and studied history. I realized there are many types of courage that don't have anything to do with combat."

"I hear that. So what do you think courage is now?" Richard was getting more interesting.

"It's the ability to face danger without succumbing to fear."

"That's concise. Without danger there is no courage. So the fear is still there but you don't let it control your actions?"

"The fear is always there. In combat it's like part of your skin or something, but you block it out, or it's part of your adrenaline rush, that tingling surge, the hyperalertness that battle requires."

"In Vietnam there was a lot of drug use among the troops. This isn't just something I read but what I've gathered from talking to veterans. What was the situation like in Iraq?"

"In Vietnam it was a serious problem, but we have a professional military now. Some men took Adderall before going out on a mission, things like that. But it was nothing compared to what students were doing at college."

I laughed. "Right, courage to face the all-night cram."

"Something like that. It's about being alert for extended periods of time. Walking into an exam unprepared can be an anxiety-fueled experience."

"Yeah, that's true. But I'd like to get back to this thing

about serving your country. In Iraq and, for that matter, Vietnam, your country, the U.S., was not endangered by these civil wars happening far away. And in Iraq U.S. actions sparked the conflict."

"Meaning?"

"Meaning that if the U.S. hadn't invaded Iraq under dubious rationale, Hussein would have remained in power. You could argue that a civil war was inevitable, but the invasion and how the occupation was administered guaranteed it."

"But Saddam Hussein was a horrible dictator."

"World-class, but so what? There's no shortage of dictators about. Should the U.S. depose them all? Most of these military adventures are just ersatz empire building, but leaving that aside, what happens afterward? Is Libya better after Gaddafi? Iraq? The point is, you don't improve the nation state by invading it with overwhelming force, smashing the infrastructure and killing the leadership. Especially when you don't have a plan for what comes after."

"All that may be true, but I do have an advantage here."

"Yes?"

"I was there."

"True that." We bumped fists. "So what's your story? Did you fight in any place I've heard of?"

"I was involved in the liberation of Fallujah."

"Liberation. I saw what 'liberation' looked like. Rubble is the word that comes to mind."

"The enemy was very difficult to dislodge."

"Probably because they lived there."

"But also, the destruction was partially due to shoddy construction."

"In other words, if it had been, say, Bonn or Oslo you were liberating, the video wouldn't have looked so bad. But never mind all that, my analysis is just thin air. What happened?"

"We were out on patrol a lot with a small unit. We had very specific objectives: generally, leaders of the opposition that we had intelligence on. If we could capture and bring them in for interrogation, we did. If there was resistance we liquidated the target. These weren't the big shots but more like local leaders."

"'Liquidated.' I find the terminology curious, like a going-out-of-business sale. But beyond that, these were Iraqis fighting an invading army, right."

"Yes. And unfortunately, there were a considerable number of questionable kills."

"'Questionable kills.' Meaning . . ."

"Civilians. Noncombatants."

"As in women, children, old folks."

Richard looked to the ground for a long time. "I witnessed atrocities. People killed merely because they were Iraqi."

"Did you participate?" I felt like a prosecutor, though I didn't want to be.

"You mean, was I the one pulling the trigger, no, I didn't. But I shouldn't have stood by without saying anything." Richard's whole stature had declined as this conversation proceeded.

"Well, Richard. A longtime and justly famed war correspondent, Chris Hedges, once wrote that physical courage on the battlefield is common. You take great risks to save each other. But moral courage in the same context is rare."

Richard gave that some thought. "I see what he means, and the two are connected. That is, the same solidarity that inspires you to risk your life also makes it difficult to critique the men in your unit. It might cause them to lose trust in you. We were in dangerous situations all the time, and your trust must be absolute. An officer can and should challenge the actions of his men, but I was just a lance corporal. You have to respect the chain of command."

"I'm sure you do. Do you think about or see those murdered civilians often?"

"Every night."

"That can't help your sleep any."

"No *(sir)*, it doesn't. I take pills sometimes. Drinking enough beer helps. But it's a chronic problem."

Night was coming on and we sat with it. I can't say what Richard was thinking about, though I can guess, but I had rotated my slippery memory back to Vietnam. I had declined to serve, but veterans who were struggling with what they had seen and done were everywhere you turned. Their transition back into civilian life was harsh and jarring. It was all fragments now, memory shrapnel tearing holes in the void.

Richard crushed a beer can. "You must think I'm some kind of monster, or moral midget."

"I'm not here to tell you what's right or wrong."

"You're not? Then what the fuck are you here for?"

"That has yet to be determined."

"You are so full of shit."

"Yeah, that's undoubtedly the case, though on a purely physical level my bowel system is solid. I rock the movement several times a day. And I squat in a different place with a view each time. In that sense I'm just processing rather than being full of."

"What is this shit?" Richard was getting frustrated.

"Okay, right and wrong. Are those the only choices?"

"What else is there?"

"An ancient Greek writer, Heraclitus, wrote, *Panta rhei,* all is flux. And that's about it, really. What else is there to say? Look at the world, everything is a blend of many things, flux, and it isn't the same as when we began talking. You and I are the product of millions of genetic decisions that we didn't have anything to do with. And that process is ongoing, it's happening right now, inside us both. So really, existence is not black and white, right or wrong, because you can't stop the flux, this process of continuous change. You can only ride it, like a wave, or a river. There's nothing to hang onto."

"But how can you live like that?"

"Maybe we can't." I shrugged. "Maybe we never understand and just stumble around until we die. It circles back around to right and wrong and that need to make judgment, to divide the world into categories. To leave that way of being behind, at least some of the time, is both the easiest and hardest way of living."

"Damn, you're not much help."

"I don't suppose I am. How do we live, that's the only question. Besides, what's for dinner?"

"You're so full of shit."

"Yeah, I suppose so. You win."

"Well then, what the fuck are you doing up here?"

"Nothing, really."

"Then what the fuck am I . . ." He stopped.

I smiled. "Your expectations are yours and you can do

with them what you want, but I can't do anything with them. I don't even have access. And tomorrow they'll be different."

"It's like a mirror or something. Whatever anyone says, you can just turn it around."

"Oh, that might be partially true. What I bring to the meeting is a willingness to be wrong, or no need to be right. I'm not saying that very well. You see, I think all human endeavor ends in failure."

"What? Then why do anything? And what do you mean, anyway?"

"Nothing lasts. Everything breaks down and ends up as dust. And, finally, death, which we can call the failure of the body."

"Okay, that's pretty good."

"You think so? Huh. You see, I don't have a static philosophy. I can't give you a program to follow. All I'm doing is trying to do is give you my full attention and then improvise with where we are now. And of course that whole identity concept is pretty wobbly. I don't invite anyone up here. Folks come because they're curious or want something or whatever. Maybe they're just lost. There are as many reasons as visitors, but everybody is carrying something up the hill. And that's like their gift."

"Gift?"

"Not like a prezzie, but more what they bring to the encounter. There was a Tibetan Buddhist teacher in America by the name of Chogyam Trungpa who had many original insights and expressed them with a very vivid imagery and metaphoric possibility. Anyway, he said that your neurosis, your problems, all that shit you've accumulated that's gurgling around in you, that gives you no rest, that stuff is the key to seeing clearly. He called it the manure of experience and said you should spread it on the field of *bohdi*. Bohdi means awareness, enlightened mind, which, the Buddhists claim, is always there, or rather, here." I snapped my fingers. "That's why they call it awakening. The idea is that you are waking up to you, or to reality, that sort of thing."

"Are you a Buddhist?"

"No. I've been around some teachers, received meditation instruction, that sort of thing, but I never signed up. They call it taking refuge where you commit yourself to follow the teachings. And you do this with a teacher, generally one you intend to study with."

"Why didn't you?"

"Oh, I could go on about certain teachings in the Buddhist tradition that I don't agree with, but really, I'm just not much of a joiner. And I would not do something like that lightly. I would take that commitment seriously. So, for instance, many years ago I was playing saxophone in a gospel band. I was playing with them because I dug the music we were making, and because I had been summoned in this really Zen kind of way. Another story, another time. We were blowing this way-out gospel. The preacher, a young guy who could really bang it out on piano, wanted me to blow free over the top of it. Well, I didn't need to be asked twice. I was also asked, every week, we were doing this in a church you understand, every week he would ask me whether I wanted to be received into the circle of faith. What this meant was that the victim, ha, that's not fair, the new member of the congregation would get up in front of people, and the preacher would do a laying on of the hands and a calling down of the spirit and accepting Jesus as your savior, all that kind of thing. I'd witnessed a few of these, but I always declined because I didn't believe. Not even close. I loathe Christianity. I was there to blow, and the rest was of no interest. So to stand up there and participate in such a ceremony felt like mockery, denigration. And I had no desire to do that. The Reverend merely asked, no pressure, he was utterly convinced that I would see the light. If people want to believe that shit, let 'er rip. We stagger through life and then we're dead, zip, kaput, nada mas. So even if these ideas of heaven, or to take the Buddhists, reincarnation, are nonsense, so what? If they help you get through the day then why not? If you are convinced, as I am, that after death there is nothing, the void, then it doesn't really make any difference how you lead your life. You get to the end no matter what. It doesn't make any difference how you lead your fucking life. There's no payoff. You don't get a merit badge for all the time you spent helping refugees or how purely organic your diet was or how you treated your mother or how much energy you used or didn't use. Or, conversely, if you spent your life killing and raping, doesn't matter. You're fucking dead and that's it. There isn't any score card, nobody is watching you except you."

He was staring, eyes boring in. "Manure, huh?"

"Yeah." I laughed. "Who's full of shit now?"

Richard laughed with me. We bumped fists again.

"So the only question is how do we live life right now?"

"Well yeah, how do we?"

This was the tilt moment. I knew how I was living it and it worked for me, but did that apply to anyone else? There weren't any other shamans fake or genuine in these hills, so it wasn't a path pursued by many. Here's a guy with, so far, functional PTSD. He wasn't even taking any pills, besides the odd sleep aid.

"Richard, when do you feel good about yourself?"

"I like sports. Working out. I really enjoying coaching the kids. That can be a blast."

"You in a relationship?"

"No. I'd like to be." He sighed. "Look, you're meeting me at my best. The two weeks here in Greece has really mellowed me out. But I can still be a little quirky and jumpy."

"A big good-looking guy like you, intelligent, job, I would think you wouldn't have any trouble attracting female attention."

"Oh, I've gone out with lots of very nice women. But we usually don't get past the third or fourth date."

"What happens?"

"They get wary or spooked, I guess. Mostly it's a 'I don't think this is gonna work out' kinda thing."

"Do you own guns?"

"Yes I do. I have a Remington Sendero for deer hunting and a .45 Beretta Px4 Storm."

"What's that?"

"A semi-automatic pistol."

"And you have that because . . ."

"I like it. I don't carry it in my truck, if that's what you're thinking."

"There were a lot of guns in the States when I left long ago and there's even more now is what I hear. Other than that, eh. There isn't a lot of gun ownership here in Greece. Hunting rifles for bird hunting. Oh, we do have wild boar in these hills."

Richard rotated his head scanning the perimeter. "Do they hunt them?"

"I believe they're trying to cull some now, as there isn't any predator to control the population. Today man is predator to man, and we have wars so we can hunt on a massive scale, a culling if you will, now that we don't hunt to eat, now that we have lost our fear of lion."

Richard stared off into the darkness, Gurdjieff did that swaying thing we attribute to elephants. May was watching a three-quarter moon rise over the Parnona with the binoculars I had given her. "Oh wow, it's so fucking clear here. I can see all the blemishes on the moon." We watched the rise together.

"Are you religious, Richard? Do you believe in a god? A supreme being, something beyond our imaginations?"

"Yeah. I don't go to a church or anything, but I believe there's something larger than us."

"And is this 'something' conscious?"

"Umm . . ."

"That's the crux really. Obviously our brief species is a speck of nothing in the vastness of the cosmos. Is there an omnipresent intelligence overseeing the whole chaotic stew?"

"When it's put that way it's hard to answer in the affirmative."

"I can dig it. How could there be a loving god overseeing this mess? I mean, one that could alter events. And a limited god is even weirder. The ancient Greeks had lots of limited gods so they could have different fields of influence. Poseidon was doing sea shit, someone else is doing wind. Kind of like patron saints."

"I guess I believe in a universal spirit kinda thing that connects us all."

"Okay, but isn't it curious that in the Western world,

and especially in the States, there's a large part of the population who believe in a vague undefined god. I'm not talking about evangelicals and the true believers, never mind them. But the regular folks who don't attend church but hang onto a belief in a Supreme Being and, if the polls are correct, fucking angels. That's just too much Marvel universe bleeding into the real world." I had, unconsciously, gotten out of my chair and was pacing in front of May and Richard, gesturing toward the stars, that sort of thing. "Most of these people have no real idea what they mean when they say they believe in a god, or God. Ta-da! No, it's just some great spirit that communes with their soul, whatever that is. I can dig it. It's a comfort thing. There's something to appeal to when the shit goes down. A loved one is sick, you pray for them. Because you are talking to the omnipresent you don't have to be near, you can send your prayers, or meditations, around the globe, to anywhere. And it's instant, I guess, the healing benefits." The moonrise was so delicately slow. "And why not? Faith and religion are there for all the shit you can't figure out. Why does something fall from my hand when I let go? I don't know, it's 'cause god wants it that way. Oh, okay, I get it. Get what? Religion is for what you don't get. Whatever makes you feel better, I'm all for it, on an individual scale. But, I think Western societies, less in Europe, are suffering from a Christian hangover. Two thousand years of this shit is way more than enough. And Islam, oh shit, it's just hitting its stride. It's got hundreds and hundreds of years to play out. You can get a headache just thinking about it. Me, like I said a few minutes ago, I think this is it. There's no god, and when we die, that's it, finito. Like there's a sign there: **NO GOING BACK. NO GOING FORWARD.**

NO SKATEBOARDING. And yet, I base this on science I don't truly understand. We choose the science myth that appeals to us. It's not like I can do the math. I can't run a few equations, crunch some numbers. and bingo, I knew there wasn't any fucking god. They say the universe is 14 billion years old. I don't know how they figure that, but what it means is that it isn't infinite. It had a beginning, maybe it has an end, though that shouldn't concern us. And they say it's curved, the edge out there. So fuck, maybe we're just in a kind of snow globe, and every few eons some being shakes it. Bang, you're flying all over the place, banging against the sky, and then everything settles down again, though that probably takes a few billion years. Is that crazier than a parallel universe? Legitimate scientists are talking this shit. Like you've got a doppelganger over in the other universe. That would explain those odd aches and pains you get. It's just your doppelganger who twisted his ankle just then. O'Keeffe, wake up, I'm talking you, girl. There's a bitch over in the parallel universe just like you. Or maybe it's a palindrome universe and dog is god over there? Oh fuck, trying to look at the universe rationally probably doesn't help. Doesn't hurt though. I'm sorry, Richard, I can't imagine you find any of this beneficial."

Great lunar shadows bent across the path. I needed a new slant. We are all reflections of light. "One of the main texts in Indian culture is the Bhagavad Gita. The name means, um, song of the lord. It's a huge, epic thing, but the main action concerns Arjuna, a warrior prince, and his charioteer, Krishna, who is actually a manifestation of the big god, Vishnu. Like the Christians say that Jesus came from God the father. And Krishna is giving Arjuna advice and teachings all the time. So there's a war going on, and Arjuna, he doesn't know if he wants to fight. Krishna insists on the necessity of action. Dude, you're a warrior, so you do the battle. This is when he introduces karma yoga, which is detachment from result. Desireless action. You just act in accordance with your duty. Those innocent people you saw killed, nothing you can do to bring them back. Their suffering is over. No more dust and bombs and terror for them."

Richard gurgled out a snore. May was slumped in the chair, her head on her shoulder. Abandoned by their gods, they had left for the land of nod, a true parallel universe where a different set of deities reign, gods that never listen and like to mix and match bits from other dimensions. They left me behind, a faux idiot yakking away to a deaf mute moon.

7: Shaman/Shamus

A cloud drifts across the blue dome of the possible as I float and stroke along the shore. A swallow swoops low and skims the sea. Weak swimmers often use the backstroke, it requires much less coordination, and you can watch the sky while moving your limbs, and sometimes something happens up there, phenomena that stand, or rather, fly in for something else. For everything in the sky is by definition flying, floating, suspended in a vastness that is not empty. That jet tracing a long, puffy line across the turquoise, what does it mean? Not only what does it mean, but how many meanings does it bear? It dates the era, certainly, and by direction it is headed south toward Crete, Cairo, Cape Town . . . somewhere. They don't launch commercial planes into space for the fun of it *and* it represents this moment, reminding me that the modern technological world is ever at hand, ever defining life and space and, too, corrupting it, poisoning it, spewing the burnt remains of dinosaur residue which are actually particles of sun. There are people in that metal tube, and they are just settling in for what may be be a very long flight, a flight such as the swallows make, sans predators. It is too high to hear and its progress across feels slow, as slow as my laborious windmilling of arms and kicking of legs. At least I don't have to think about floating, any more than they have to think about flying. Why are they flying to Cairo? Or Tripoli? What rendezvous has summoned them to tear across the Mediterranean sky toward uncertain fates and indifferent food? As the song goes, *"There may be trouble ahead, but while there's moonlight and love and romance, let's face the music and dance."* Or swim.

And still the plane crawls across the blue. How is the pilot feeling today? Did he fuck some stewardess during the Athens layover, or did he take in the Archaeological Museum? Maybe he spent an hour staring into the golden face of Agamemnon while pondering the fate of kings? Maybe his Clytemnestra awaits him in Jo'burg? And even this moment is plotting his demise, though probably not with a sword. How do the white folks do it down there? Oh yes, they fire a revolver repeatedly through a locked bathroom door in self-defense. Perhaps there's a murderer aboard, or a saint? Odds favor the former. Saints are thin on the ground. Or in the air, for that matter. What's the difference between murderer and killer? I suppose I mean, when I say killer, someone who has killed in the line of duty: military, law enforcement, that sort of thing. And there are positions in organized crime that require you to eliminate someone, that's a job too, whereas murderer implies a personal edge to the violence. Obviously there's considerable overlap in my definitions. When Michael kills Freddo it's personal *and* in the line of duty. And you can kill for a cause, the revolution and its various mutations. And there are the rare examples of homicide in self-defense. And there's accidental homicide, you get drunk and crash into a station wagon and kill an entire family. You're a killer, but are you a murderer? And now we have, especially in the States for some reason, people who kill strangers, sometimes lots of them, for no apparent reason. They are murderers for sure even though they didn't know the victims. It's great luck to have never faced these situations and had to decide. Some passengers have probably already fallen asleep, the swine. Wake me up when we're over South Sudan, I'm curious what that level of suffering looks like from thirty thousand feet. Is it any different than on TV? TV is both much closer and far more distant—disembodied comes to mind, or beyond that, spectral. Maybe there's a civil war channel on the in-flight entertainment system? Will we be able to see the child miners in Congo digging up coltan for our phones? Bless their hearts, what would we do without them? And I hear they do it for free.

A large majority of the planetary population has never been in a plane, yet we take it for granted. It's easier than walking to the next village. Homo sapiens has always floated. Perhaps they floated in when land began to form? Each time I bring an arm overhead for the next stroke it unleashes a spray of water that the sun prisms as it separates into drops falling. This takes less than a second, the arc of arm and resultant rainbow. And then there's another. The sea grants your resistance to gravity a grace and flow that most of us rarely know. I glance toward shore, and here comes Stein, who has tired of running along the beach. She's an excellent swimmer. I have to quicken my pace in order to keep abreast of her. She tends to turn into me if I don't keep up. A herding instinct. But I can't keep up the sprint very long, and after fifty meters I push her toward shore and stagger onto the sand.

It's a midweek day in July and the small beach is empty. I hear a hawk's cry, roll onto my back, and catch it disappearing over a nearby hill. Stein is digging a hole. I have a campsite thirty meters off the beach in an olive orchard. It doesn't amount to much: a small tent, a chair, a chest to keep food, a petro gas cooker to heat water, and a hammock for meditation. I spent most the summer here.

The rest of the dogs and Gurdjieff were at my house in the mountains. I let a friend stay there, and she took care of them. It would have been too difficult to bring them all. Many people find a pack of dogs intimidating, and it was best to avoid the hassle. I brought Stein because she was the easiest and the smartest. I returned every week for a day or two. They were used to it and adjusted quickly.

I was reading Nadezhda Mandelstam's *Hope Against Hope* that week, and it was a grim read. The weather in Russia would bum me out, but to endure it while living in Stalin's state of terror . . . I was halfway through the thick tome and coming to the conclusion that lighter fare was in order. Stein leapt up and barked out a warning. I looked, and up from the beach came my old friend Diogenes with a bag o' beer. Lovely, save for an unusual dark vibe he brought with him.

Diogenes was a pomegranate and olive farmer, musician, entrepreneur, and a beloved character locally. He knew everybody and was adored by dogs. He vigorously stroked Stein's head. "Hey Stein, how are you, girl?" She confirmed her well-being with rapid tail movement.

"Say brother, you are a welcome sight. *And* you are bearing beer. How very nice."

"Hey Max, things look pretty calm here."

"No reason why they shouldn't. Got the beach, sun, Stein, and some literature. And now beer. Next thing you know you'll produce some beautiful eager woman. Don't fucking wake me up."

Diogenes scanned the olive orchard. He shook his head, spit, lit a smoke. "Being here you'd never guess what's going on in Vathi."

I popped a beer, handed it to my friend, and opened

one for myself. We touched cans. "Something tells me bad weather is en route."

"It's chaos over there, man. Pericles is dead. He was found in the walk-in refrigerator at the campground restaurant kitchen."

"What? Did someone or . . . oh fuck, tell me what you know."

"That's the weird part. He was found in the fridge this morning when folks came in to start prepping lunch, naked and curled up under a shelf."

"Did you see the body?"

"No, no I didn't, but Panayioti's brother Kosta is a cop, and I got this from Panayioti. And what he tells me is there aren't any signs of violence."

"The fridge was unlocked?"

"Yeah. Closed, but unlocked."

"What are they thinking?"

"Well, it's real early, but they're thinking he died of cold, of . . ."

"Hypothermia."

"Yeah, right, hypothermia."

"Something about that doesn't sound right. I mean, how they found the body is consistent with hypothermia. For some reason people suffering from moderate to severe hypothermia often nude up, take all their clothes off. It's called 'paradoxical undressing.' And the curling up under the shelf is also consistent with this."

"Really? How do you know this stuff?"

"Back in the States I had friends who worked in mountain/wilderness rescue, and they often dealt with hypothermia. So I picked up a few things, some of the vocabulary. But what was he doing in an unlocked walk-in? I mean, that would be a long, weird suicide, especially as when the discomfort got worse you could just walk out."

"It's very strange. There must be more to the story."

"Can the walk-in be locked from outside?"

Diogenes shook his head. "I don't know. Maybe. I've never worked in that kitchen."

"Could you find out?"

"I know where the key to the back door is. Late tonight we could look if you want."

"The restaurant is closed, I assume."

"For sure, and I don't think it will open. Pericles is the one who took out the contract to run it for the summer. No one else will do it now."

"Damn. I liked Pericles. I'll miss him. Why not, let's take a look at the kitchen."

Sometime after midnight we slipped up to the back door that opened onto a gravel lot. There were dumpsters and crates of empty beer bottles and various assorted crap piled about. We could hear music from the Kronos café bar. Screaming Jay Hawkins was shouting out, *I'll put a spell on you.* I turned and whispered to Diogenes, "Who put a spell on Pericles?" *Stop the things you do, I ain't lying.* He nodded grimly. Stein was busying herself with the bouquet of scents available. No one could see us, and Diogenes extracted the key from beneath a concrete block.

I had a small flashlight and D. used his phone as we entered, listening intently. Stein raced past us and began examining the floor with her nose. The kitchen was walled off from the front of the place so there was little chance our lights would be seen. The work stations, shelves, and counters, mostly stainless steel, were cleaned and empty.

The walk-in was closed, and we stood before it and examined the latch mechanism. "There you go," I said, "you can lock it from the outside. You could put a padlock through these holes here and that would secure it. You know, if you were worried about people stealing food after hours, which is common enough."

Diogenes was running his light along the door. "Looks like a pretty good seal on this thing."

"There's a way to check that." I walked over to the ovens and found an oven mitt. Using it, I opened the walk-in door. We both almost expected to see Pericles on the floor and were relieved we didn't. It was about two meters deep and a bit less than a meter and a half wide. It had been turned off but there were still foodstuffs on the shelves: tubs of tzadziki, blocks of cheese, various translucent plastic containers with things like tomatoes and lemons. There was an empty fruit juice container on the floor. "He didn't die of thirst, anyway."

We turned and looked at the inside of the door. There was a disk attached to a rod that passed through the door. You could push it to open the door if it had been closed while you were in it. There wasn't much to see and no signs of a struggle. "This is a grim fucking place to spend your last hours. Pericles, what the fuck were you doing? I don't get it." I looked down at the dog. "You find anything, Stein?" She wagged her tail and exited. "Dio, could you close the door, I just want to see what it's like. Here, use the mitt." The door closed and the space violently contracted. I turned off my light. It was a vacuum, you couldn't hear a thing, and the darkness was complete. I spoke in a loud voice, "Dio, can you hear me?" Nothing. Turning my flashlight back on, I grabbed a cloth off a shelf and pushed the opening mechanism. The door popped open. Relief. "Did you hear me in there?"

Diogenes shook his head. "Not a sound."

"Okay. Let's close the door again, and I'm going to shine my light along the edges of the door starting on the lower corner on the hinge side and going clockwise. You turn your light out and follow along to see if there's any light coming through. Let me see if I can close this myself just pulling on this handle thing." It was difficult but I managed to close it.

We stood in the kitchen without a clue. I started thinking out loud. "So there's two entrances, the back door and through these swinging saloon doors out to the dining room and the patio. There are no signs of theft or of violence, right?"

"That's what Panayioti said. And I can't see anything wrong."

"Neither can I, but come on, I don't believe Pericles committed suicide by closing himself in the walk-in. You want it to be swift, like with a gun, or at least painless, pills or slit wrists in the bathtub, but by hypothermia? Okay, maybe they do it that way in Norway or Finland, but this is fucking Greece!"

"You know, at first I was almost ready to believe it, what the cops were saying, but you've convinced me it must have been something different."

"Let's get out of here and have a beer."

Near the back door Stein nudged something near the floor. I directed my light. She was licking something on the bottom shelf. I bent over and found a meat thermometer. "Is there any flavor on that, girl?" What was it doing here when the ovens were at the other end of the room? "Dio, I'll be right out, hold on for a second." I walked back to the fridge door. I took the thermometer and slid it through the lock holes. A good fit. The round gauge at the end kept it from falling through. I pulled it out and put it back on the same shelf as I exited.

We clicked bottles of Pilsner and drank. The Kronos café bar was about fifty meters from the restaurant and amounted to a bamboo canopy over a concrete slab littered with tables and chairs. A small river ran by it and cut through the sandy beach to the sea. We looked out across the beach to the bay. It was dark and still. There were twenty or so others gathered around tables, a mix of locals and tourists from Western Europe. Leonard Cohen was moaning over us. *Everybody knows the good guys lost.*

"Dio, you knew Pericles quite well, didn't you?"

"My whole life. Same village, same age, we went to school together. Hell, we were even in the army together. And we're still good friends. Or we were, I guess." Diogenes tapped another cigarette from his pack and lit it. We ate the complimentary peanuts. "And we both spent time up in Germany, near Nuremberg."

Germany. Young German women come to Greece for the holidays, have a torrid affair with a Greek guy, and decide they're in love and wish to be twained with the dark handsome barefoot guy hanging out at the beach. He's so much fun. They have no way of knowing that that guy will still be hanging out at the beach twenty years later, when they need something more than fun. Did I say twenty years? It usually takes less than ten, and then they pack up the kids and head back to Deutschland, where they finish their education degree and start teaching while the parents watch the grandchildren. There's a certain cycle, like migratory birds. From each generation Northern Europe sacrifices a certain number of maidens to Zeus on the beaches of the Aegean. Hey, mix up the gene pool. And remember, not only is it not fatal, it's all voluntary. The kids are often beautiful. Diogenes's wife Petra was there with their two daughters.

"Both our wives and kids are up there."

"In the same town?"

"Yeah, Petra and Ursula are good friends. They came to Greece together the first time."

"What, you and Pericles met your future wives together, here, on this beach?"

Diogenes gave me a sheepish grin and nodded. "Yeah, we did. At first we were with the other one, and then one drunken night we switched and everything clicked. That was a great summer."

"I'll bet it was. Sounds like you and Pericles were joined at the hip or something."

"You could say he was my best friend."

Pericles was a tall, good-looking guy in his late forties. Well loved, he was an archetype for men of his age from farming/working-class backgrounds in the beach communities of Lakonia. He harvested the family olive orchards in the winter, sold firewood, did construction when it was available, and worked in the small, sleepy tourist business in the summer. When he was younger he bartended, waited tables, the usual. Running the campground restaurant was a more ambitious undertaking. He spoke excellent English and passable German and played a powerful electric bass. Diogenes hosted a jam session in the barn at his farm every Monday night. I sat in when I was around. What happened to Pericles?

They're postponing the funeral for a couple of days so Ursula and their kids can attend."

"They're in Germany?"

"Yeah. I was the one who called Ursula. She was screaming into the phone. They fly to Athens tomorrow. Petra and my girls are coming too. They all loved Pericles."

I reached over and caressed Diogenes shoulder but the tears came anyway. He got me going as well, and we wept together for our fallen friend. How could he not be sitting with us this very moment? I looked up to see others at a nearby table weeping into their beers. It was a sad café playing very sad music.

When did you last see him?" The whole thing was very disturbing.

"Last night. *Gahmoto!* Right here at the bar. We were planning on playing a concert here on the beach later this month."

"How did he seem?"

"Good. Same as always. Laughing, drinking beer, you know."

"Not presuicidal. What time was that?"

"From about nine to eleven, I think. I left about then."

"Did the police interview you today?"

"Yeah, they did. Before I came over to you."

"And?"

"They kept asking about drugs and stuff like that. Was he depressed and how things were going for him."

"Drugs? Was he doing anything interesting?"

"Nah, smoking pot like the rest of us, but nothing else. I would know."

"The autopsy will tell us the drug story. And maybe plenty else. When will that happen?"

"Panayioti said it would happen today."

"Good, 'cause I don't buy the suicide narrative."

"Neither do I, man, but what can we do?"

What could we do? We didn't have a clue. But this was the story, and we were already well into it. "Dio, I'm going to move my tent over here and hang out for a few days, talk to people, think about it. Next time you talk to Panayioti, ask him to find out for sure that the walk-in door was unlocked. I mean, it must have been or the cops would be talking homicide, you would think. Oh, wait a minute, who found him?"

"Eleni. You know her. Long black hair, pretty good-looking, about thirty."

"Yeah, I know her to say hello. I don't think we can depend on the Gythio cops. They'll want to close the case so they can spend their time ogling babes on the beach. Though, to be fair, there don't appear to be any clues. And keep thinking about Pericles, anything that might explain this."

"That's all I'm doing, man. I can't think of anything else."

Cohen's *Hallelujah* disappeared into the warm balmy evening.

I broke camp the next morning, and Stein and I set up just down the beach from the Kronos bar and campsite. It wasn't a hardship. Vathi has one of the most beautiful beaches in Lakonia, and except for August there's plenty of room for everyone. Stein loved it as there were plenty of dogs about. Most of the day she spent with her canine companions, but she always knew where I was and would swing by for a few minutes every hour or two. Much as a child would. Diogenes and I met for coffee each morning and tried to think together.

"Hey Max, I'm going up to the village to pay my respects to the family, you want to come."

"Certainly. I'm all in on this story."

The family lived in a small Mani village atop a hill that afforded panoramic views in all directions including down a narrow valley to the sea. Mountains and rolling hills and olive trees, everywhere olives. The house was an old stone Mani house. Attached was part of an ancient tower in partial collapse. Pericles's family had been here for many generations. Although it was late morning it was already hot as a muthafucka. Much of the village was milling about in the *platea* when we drove up. Diogenes knew everyone and was met with tearful embraces and whispers. The air was rife with anguish and rumor and innuendo. Death can bring out the worst in a Greek village, as though all the demons, representing decades of bitterness and envy, are released into the atmosphere to swirl about staining the community until the body is interred in the earth, whereupon they settle back and wait for the next departing spirit.

We shook hands, hugged, murmured platitudes as we made our way toward Pericles's family home, which occupied a corner of the *platea*. It was another brilliant sunny summer morning, and besides your narrator, anyone who had ever smoked was smoking today. As we ascended an old stone staircase I could hear something that resembled chanting, but when we arrived at the top, where a large covered veranda occupied one side of the house, I was relieved to see not *papas* but *yiayias*, old Mani women keening.

Mani is famed for the artistry of its mourning. The women, exclusively women, chant out an improvised poetry that is sung from the back of the throat, similar to some Native American singing. Some of it is generic mourning imagery, but the good ones also tell the tale of the deceased. There used to be many professional mourners throughout the peninsula who could be hired to escort your beloved to the next world with verse. One woman would sing out an eight-bar phrase and then another would pick it up. Incense was burning. It was unnervingly intense, even though I could hardly understand a word. It was as though the crones were summoning the *Erinyes*, the Furies, to pursue the guilty one. The dead man's younger sister Eleftheria was holding herself and rocking in a chair. An old village guy, dark leathery skin, cap pulled down, cigarette smoking beneath his bristly mustache, would occasionally hit a drum he was holding. Just an odd seemingly random thump. Normally the body would be in an open casket on a table surrounded by the women, but due to the delay, allowing his wife and children time to return, the corpse was in a refrigeration unit somewhere. In this heat the corpse wouldn't have made it to the funeral. The thought passed that they could have just left him in the walk-in, a whimsy I didn't share.

Nobody really wanted to talk to me, and I slid to the background and studied the crowd while Diogenes wept with the women. Did anyone here know anything? I had come to the conclusion, barring something unforeseen from the as yet unreleased autopsy, that Pericles had been deliberately locked in the walk-in. This would mean that this person, or someone else, would have had to come back in the morning to unlock it, by which time Pericles was just chilled meat. My criminal narrative was pretty loose, but that was the only story that made any sense. With this story the death could, conceivably, be accidental. That is, maybe someone just wanted to fuck with Pericles for a while, but when they returned he'd already breathed his last. Or it was deliberate, and the perp had returned after he'd estimated that ole Pericles was kaput, to unlock and cover his tracks, which was pretty ingenious when you think about it, and mostly definitely premeditated. If that was the case, it would have to be someone who knew Pericles's habits intimately, would know that he always checked the walk-in when he was doing his after-hours rounds. Not only that, but they would have to be close behind him in order to spring into action as soon as he entered the fridge. I figure thirty seconds max, unless he was doing inventory. We hadn't seen anything that smacked of inventory-taking in the walk-in, a clipboard with a printed graph on it, that sort of thing. Maybe the police had found something. There could be more than one murderer. Or the murderer may have met Pericles in the kitchen, argued over money or a woman perhaps, and then Pericles had dismissed him, but maybe her, and entered the walk-in, whereupon the door slammed shut. I hadn't laid this theory on anyone yet, but later I'd run it by Diogenes. Was the murderer here right now?

So, what do we do now? I mean, we don't have any evidence, do we?" Diogenes didn't like the sound of murder, especially in this instance, where a killer was known, but not, and among us. Neither did I.

"I don't know. Let's keep this idea between us for now. No sense stirring people up when all we've got is a story we've invented. Let's wait until the autopsy. Maybe it's as simple as a drug overdose."

"Who takes an overdose of drugs and then closes themselves in a refrigerator and takes their clothes off?"

"Exactly," I asked, "who is that person?"

"Not Pericles, that's for sure."

Besides swimming and reading, I spent most of the day and night talking and listening, either on the beach or at a table in the Kronos café or at the Blue Beach, another café some fifty meters down the beach. I kept it casual and only made notes after each conversation. Stories, some first-person, others second-hand, floated in like flotsam. Most had nothing to do with Pericles.

The autopsy showed no sign of dangerous drugs. Marijuana and alcohol, of course. Now they're trying to say he fell down drunk in the walk-in."

"But first he pulled the door closed behind him and got naked. What the fuck."

We were at the café, late morning, doing coffee. The sea was calm, life was already moving on. I had talked to Eleni. She was an emotional mess but had no insight save to confirm that the walk-in was shut, not locked, and the back and front doors were locked.

"Yeah, I know. And his alcohol reading was only .15.

Which is enough to get you a DUI, but it hardly means you're staggering falling-down drunk. I think three beers can get you there. Nearly anyone leaving this café at night would blow a .15.

"True that. But that amount of alcohol combined with how lightly he was dressed greatly increased the chances of death from hypothermia. A sober, warmly dressed man would stand a decent chance of surviving that time in the walk-in. You know, most of the time, fuck, near all the time, I enjoy living in a country where the enforcement of the law is casual, something that is easy to ignore, but there comes the moment when you want real police. Where are those TV detectives when you need them?"

We sipped. Petra and Ursula, having arrived late yesterday, were at a table of foreign women who lived in the area. Their children were at another table with their Greek peers. "Dio, we need a motive. Someone who had a beef with Pericles. Someone who felt he had screwed them over. Money. Romantic betrayal. That kind of thing. Oh, I talked to Eleni. I saw her on the beach this morning. Her dog was playing with Stein. She's a fucking wreck. She didn't give me anything new. She came in in the morning, started her regular routine, opened the walk-in, and there he was. It was hard to get her to talk. She was weeping and gagging. Oh, she did say something weird. You know we were wondering about whether he was doing inventory. She said she found the clipboard with the inventory sheet on a shelf in the walk-in and put it back on a hook on the wall near the little office table in the corner of the kitchen. I asked her why she did that, and she just said it didn't belong in the walk-in."

We watched the dogs wrestling on the sand. I looked

down at my notebook where I had jotted questions. "Had Pericles fired anyone this summer? I can't imagine it, but the restaurant business, hell, it happens all the time."

Diogenes nodded his head. "Actually, he had. He talked about it with me. It was two or three weeks ago. Miltiades, you know him, I think. He's a regular around here. A really nice guy and lots of fun, but he drinks too much and can't make it to work. He gets fired from jobs all the time. But everyone likes him, and so someone else hires him, often the same people who fired him the year before. Not much of a suspect, but I guess it's something. He's from over by Selinitsa originally." He put out his smoke. "So far I haven't come up with anything. Like I said, he didn't have a steady girlfriend . . ."

"Wasn't that unusual? Didn't he always have . . . female companionship?"

"You could say the same about you, and here you are."

"Fair enough. So no steady gal. He's still married to Ursula, isn't he? I mean, I know she lives in Germany, but . . ."

"They had an open marriage kinda thing. They saw other people, but he went up there once or twice year, and they always spent part of the summer here."

"Some would call that ideal, but I wouldn't want to be that absent from my children's lives. Anyone he's seen lately. I'm just fishing here."

"I don't know. I think there's at least one. Let me ask Sula."

Sula owned and ran the Kronos café and liked to know everyone's business. I'm not sure what she thought of me.

"What time is the funeral?"

Diogenes lit another smoke. "Around three, I guess.

That's when the *papas* will start to chant anyway. The coffin with Pericles is being taken to the church now, and so the family will be there, I would think."

"You'll be taking the wife and kids up, I imagine."

"We could squeeze you in."

"Don't worry about it. I'll either drive myself or catch a ride with someone. Isn't about half the population of this area going?"

"There'll be a lot of people. With the delay of the funeral plenty of people who couldn't have made it have been able to make arrangements. Lots of people from Athens will be there."

"Where's the wake or reception, whatever they call it?"

Diogenes thought for a moment. "I can't think of the word right now, but it's at Maria's."

I caught a ride with Shrink Dogg. "Where's your son, Dogg?"

"Aliki is watching all of the kids at the beach. They don't need exposure to all this grief."

"How much is enough?"

He turned from the road. "Huh? Enough of what?"

"Loss."

"I believe we are capable of enduring a great deal of it. In May I volunteered out on Mytilini, working with the Syrian refugees. I encountered people who had lost ten family members: sisters, brothers, children. Horrible, violent situations. And still they got up every morning and made a cup of tea. It would have been better if I spoke French."

"We would all benefit from that." I was watching the olive trees flow past.

"Speaking French?"

"Expanded capacity for loss."

Shrink Dogg laughed. "Still being cryptic, I see. What do you think about Pericles's death? Doesn't the whole thing feel odd? What do the police think?"

"I can't speak for the police, though their investigation doesn't appear to be very aggressive. It does seem that they would prefer to treat it as accident/suicide. That way the case is, essentially, closed."

"Pericles was not suicidal. He didn't display any signs of depression. I spoke with him the day before this event. He was in good spirits, the restaurant was doing okay, or well enough. You know how it is down here. He was going to try some Mexican dishes."

"Mexican?"

"Yeah, you know, tacos, nachos, maybe burritos or something."

"Hand food. We'll never know now. About the only thing we know is that Pericles has checked out." We slowed to a stop. "What the fuck?" Though we were a kilometer from the village, the narrow road that led to it was now lined with parked cars.

S.D. swung the car onto the shoulder. "We'd better park here and walk."

The heat was terrific, pulsing off the asphalt. The cicadas were screaming, and on the road there were many mourners slowly, dutifully trudging up the hill, murmuring to each other and wiping the sweat from their foreheads. "Fucking Jesus it's hot. We might need a multiple funeral the way some of these old folks are flagging. Where's the valet service when you need it?" I have never been more grateful for the Panama on my head. It felt strange and confining wearing trousers, but you don't wear shorts to bury the dead, not even in informal Greece. The sea in the distance was like a taunt, a reminder that after the weeping and wailing we could immerse ourselves and float without thought.

The church occupied the middle of the *platea*, which was full of mourners, many crowded under the shade of several huge plane trees. From the church came the sound of priests intoning. At affairs such as this most folks don't actually stand in the church during the service. They enter the church, light a candle, maybe place a flower in the open coffin, and then exit and stand outside smoking, especially the men. I usually take a last look at the dead. It was shoulder to shoulder inside, and I followed others pushing through to the coffin.

The incense, candlelight, and chanted prayers were dizzying after the brilliant light outside. To the left of the coffin, all in black, sat the immediate family: mom, his sister Eleftheria, his brother Manolis, Ursula and their children Andreas and Sonia, and an ancient crone who might have been the *yiayia*. I spied Eleni nearby, gushing tears and whimpering. The final box was full of flowers leaving only his head exposed. Pericles, only hours from the fridge, looked fresher than the living. My turn came, and I placed a hand on the top of his head, and that got the tears going. I leaned over and kissed him on the forehead which was cold and soft. I felt like whispering a question, but maybe he didn't even know who locked him in. He certainly didn't know now. I nodded to the family and pushed my way out.

I found a place on a wall to sit and watch. In the crowd

were many people down from the city. Petra was with a cluster of women beneath one of the trees, and there were Diogenes's beautiful daughters Electra and Athena, young women now and chic in their short black dresses. I was remembering them as children when my gaze was broken by the hulking forms of Manolis and Andreas. I slid off the wall and gave them the obligatory hugs.

"I'm sorry guys, I don't know what to say. It's an awful day we won't forget." They were both looking rather intently at me, especially the son, Andreas, who spoke.

"What do you think happened to my father?"

I stifled a groan. Diogenes, *gahmoto*. I should have known. I looked Andreas in the eye. Intense, teary, trying to man-up to catastrophe, he was a wonderful synthesis of his parents, tall and lean with piercing blue eyes and wavy brown hair. "First off, Andre, I don't know anything more than you do." I shrugged. "That said, I also have doubts that your father's sad demise was self-inflicted."

"Why?"

"I don't think anyone, especially your father, goes into a refrigerator and chills himself to death. Once you come to that conclusion, you start to ask how, how did he end up naked in the walk-in?"

Andreas and Manolis stood before me unblinking, waiting, though I don't think Manolis understood much English.

"The only thing that makes sense, not that much, but anyway, someone must have locked him in and then, in the morning, unlocked it so that it looked accidental or suicidal. The death from hypothermia is quite possible given how lightly dressed he was, and he'd had something to drink, which hastens the effects of the chill." I shrugged, again. I hadn't anticipated this encounter. Fucking Diogenes.

"So who did it?" Andreas was getting wound up.

"I can't figure out a motive or a suspect. I have nothing to offer on that count."

A man tapped Manolis on the shoulder and signaled with his head toward the church. It was time to carry their loved one to his final resting place. I looked toward the church. There was a line of people going in one door and another coming out. It was time to pay last respects before the funeral procession.

The pallbearers had to duck and dance to get the coffin out the church door. Medieval Greeks must have been tiny, the doors on the buildings are really short. They straightencd up, Diogenes was a bearer, got the box settled on their shoulders, the *papas* got out in front, and they set off for the cemetery. The crowd filled in behind them, murmuring, clicking their worry beads, watching each other. I joined the procession maybe thirty meters behind the coffin, which from this distance appeared to be floating, bobbing and rocking on a human river that flowed down the narrow streets of the village lined with buildings and walls of stone, everything covered in dust and bending in the heat.

The cemetery clung to the back of the village, away from the sea and above a deep wild ravine. In the distance the Tayegetos Mountains carved the horizon jagged. The cicadas screamed, and by the time I reached the cemetery the crowd was twenty deep around the freshly dug grave. Pericles was being planted in the family plot, which was a low marble affair with headstone that had a small display cupboard where photos and totems of the lives lived could be displayed. When another died, as they always do, the large marble lid was removed and the dirt dug out for the next. Then every few years the dead were dug up and their bones placed in a tin in a small building on the cemetery grounds. This way the family could use the plot over and over. In the marble lid were carved the names and dates of the dead.

Most all the graves were covered in white marble that flashed in the sun, the air was still and burning, and the *papas* shook their incense and beseeched their god. In English cemeteries you often see sentiments such as *Gone to his final reward* or *She rests with the angels,* that sort of thing, carved in the headstones. You never see that sentiment expressed in a Greek graveyard. The culture doesn't appear to have much belief in an afterlife. I applaud their doubt.

I found a spot on the high side of the cemetery and watched from there. After the priests intoned for a bit, they took some olive oil and poured it over the body. Then the chaps struggled to lower the still-open coffin into the hole. My experience tells me this struggle is obligatory, as it invariably occurs amidst much shouting, scrambling, and sliding. Sometimes they almost tip out the stiff. Once they've got him settled in the hole, a man unties his hands, which had been bound at the wrists for the funeral. I always like that bit, as though he might need to use those hands later—not, one hopes, in a buried-alive horror fashion but rather swimming the chilled waters of the Styx, perhaps. After the hands are freed, the lid is placed on the box and the show is over. Probably because I've seen it done in movies (filmmakers love funerals: the black-clad mourners, the thick intense expanse of green, the boiling-over family tensions, the pecking order and protocol), I usually grab a handful of dirt and toss it on the coffin. It's the last goodbye, that rattle of clay and stone on the thin wood of the box lid.

Maria's taverna was a few kilometers from the village, down in the valley near the sea, which meant that a huge exodus of cars serpentined down the hill. There was always someone who had parked facing uphill but was too impatient to drive up and turn around in the village and instead insisted on attempting to turn around in the road, which added to the chaos: horns honking, fists shaken, nothing somber about it.

Maria's had a large covered open-air dining room, but given the anticipated crowd they had run tables out under the olives trees in the parking lot. That's what you do when someone in your family dies, you feed everyone who knew them. Sure, you can be cheap and just give them coffee, brandy, and a biscuit, but Pericles's clan was going for the full boat. Soon the place was packed, and servers were racing from the kitchen with salads, cheese, potatoes, and wine.

We were standing under an olive tree with glasses of wine in our hands. "Dio, I gotta tell ya, man. You fucked up. I'm sorry, I love you, brother, but you fucked up."

"Huh? What?"

"Who did you tell about our suspicions concerning Pericles's death?"

"Oh, yeah, I told Petra. I had to tell Petra."

"But Petra told Ursula, and on and on. Look around these tables, probably half the fucking people here have now heard some version of the story, because this is now a story we can't control. Every time it's passed to another it mutates. You know how it works. Pretty soon one of us will be the prime suspect. Fucking A."

"Oh, I see what you mean. Sorry about that. My bad."

"It could be worse. At least we didn't have a suspect, 'cause they'd probably be planning a lynching for after the feast if we had. The desire to punish runs deep. Andreas and Manolis talked to me just before you guys carried Pericles away. Andreas was all ready to extract revenge, for fuck sake. All our conversations on this matter have to remain confidential. That means you can't tell anyone."

Diogenes hung his head. "I understand now, it's just that Petra asked me what I thought, and, well, I should have kept my mouth shut. You thought of anything else?"

We watched the crowd eating and drinking. "No, I haven't." And I probably wouldn't tell you if I had.

"Look, there's Katina. She's just sitting down at that table."

A stout young woman in a long black dress with short spiky hair dyed an aggressive red was settling herself at the end of a table.

"Who is Katina?"

"She worked at the restaurant too. Maybe we should talk to her?"

"She worked at the restaurant? Fucking A, man, I get the information drip by fucking drip. Didn't the Chinese have some method of torture that involved drips? Myth, probably. But by all means, let's talk to Katina. Lead on."

There was a chair opposite Katina that I took, and Diogenes, who knew her, of course, pulled up a chair next to her. Diogenes greeted her with a hug and a kiss, then introduced me.

"Oh, I know who you are. You're American, with a dog, right?"

"Correct on both counts."

Diogenes plunged in. "We're trying to figure out how this whole thing went down, you know. You worked in the kitchen didn't you?"

"Oh my god, poor Pericles! How did it happen? How did he get stuck in the walk-in?" She grabbed some fries and shoved them in her mouth.

"We don't know."

"And oh my god, poor Eleni! What incredibly bad luck or what?"

"Bad luck?"

"Well, I'm always the first person in in the morning. Eleni always arrives at least twenty minutes after I do, often more than that. The first time she gets there early, she finds Pericles! Oh my god, I mean, I feel sorry for her and everything, but I am so glad it wasn't me. That would be so fucking awful. I would still be puking." She pushed a chunk of bread laden with tzatziki in her mouth. "Does that make me a bad person or something, feeling that way?"

"I don't think so. Just bad luck all around."

"When did you arrive at the restaurant?" Enough with the retching.

"Same time I always do, nine o'clock. And the police were already there!"

"Really? They must have gotten there fast."

"I guess. I hadn't thought of that."

"When did Eleni call them?"

"I don't know." She drank wine. "When she found the body, when else? Right after vomiting, I would think."

I took a drink too. "That's probably it. Corpse, puke, cops."

Katina gave me a quick, hard look, then said, "And

133

now I've got to find another fucking job, at this point in the summer." She looked around guiltily. "Oops, I shouldn't talk about that now."

Hours later I was digging my feet in the sand after a long swim. We were entering the magic twilight hour where everything went vaguely pastel for a while. It was a curious contrast to the sharp, hard-edged colors that Greece normally wears. Stein was tearing around chasing another dog. I looked down the beach and saw three attractive but somber women walking this way. Ursula, Petra, and Eleftheria arrived and sat down next to me.

"How's everyone bearing up?"

"Not very well."

"It sucks."

"Yeah, I can dig it."

Ursula turned herself toward me and fixed me with a stare. "Do you know anything about Pericles's death? I mean, anything extra, something we don't know."

I shrugged. "I don't think so. It doesn't look right, dying in the walk-in like that. I mean, it certainly looks like he died from hypothermia, but how? Did someone close him in? That's the only thing that makes sense, but I haven't got a clue. I have no suspects, suspicious persons, that kind of thing. There's just something weird about it. You now know what I know, which is next to nothing."

Ursula leaned toward me. "So the person who closed him in there is walking around right now? Maybe even on this beach?"

"Um, yeah. Once you decide it wasn't accidental, that's the conclusion you come to. But . . ." I gave them the palms-up.

"Who would do such a thing? Pericles didn't have any enemies!" Eleftheria was quivering and pawing the sand with one hand.

Ursula nodded. "That's true. I can't think of another person I could say that about. Sexual fidelity wasn't his thing, but then, it isn't mine either. But he didn't screw people over, and he was a regular working guy, nobody envied him. Unless it was because he was loved by women."

"You guys know him far better than I do, obviously, but what you say is always how I viewed him, though I never really considered him in these terms until now. He was a guy I drank beer with, played music with, that sort of thing, whose company I enjoyed. But not someone whose life I thought about with any degree of concentration."

We watched some children run along the beach followed by the dogs. Swallows were skimming along the quiet sea. Ursula rolled and lit a cigarette, then passed the tobacco to Petra.

Ursula exhaled, looked at her smoke, and said, "I gave this shit up two years ago. I've smoked two packs in the last two days." She shook her head wearily, then asked me, "You lost your wife years ago, didn't you?"

"Yes, I did. But there wasn't anything sudden about it. She was sick for years and years."

"That's what I heard. And then, what happened?"

"She died two weeks before the kids were due to leave for university, which they did. So although her dying was prolonged, the aloneness that followed felt sudden. I was definitely thrown off stride, staggered, you could say. But it all just keeps rolling along. I visited old friends who were scattered about the world, and they were gracious and eager to take me in, provide comfort and solace. And that

135

was lovely. I was very tender and open to their solicitations. And I was busy artistically due to several projects coming to fruition not long after her demise, which was a good thing." Those times were fading, sepia-toned and curling at the edges. "Within months I was on my feet and fully engaged, much as I ever am. Really, after caring for her intensely the last years, and especially the last two, there was also a powerful sense of release. All the energy I had devoted to caring for her, gladly, was still available to me, I could direct it anywhere I wanted, and I had lots of time to do it. Extended mourning would be a waste of that power. I don't know about all this honoring the dead activities. The only place they exist is in your head. They may exist in the memories of others, but it isn't the same person that's in yours. And that memory swiftly becomes our own creation, because they are just dust."

Ursula nodded, staring out at the sea. "*So ist das Leben.*"

"*Es muss sein.*"

I left the women and walked back toward Kronos in the mauve twilight world. It was still quite warm, now it felt perfect. Especially with the sea to my left washing over my feet. Diogenes was coming toward me.

"Hey Max, what's happening?"

"I just left Ursula, Petra, and Eleftheria down the beach a ways."

"How are they doing?"

"As well as can be expected. Still processing the whole thing."

"I just saw Miltiades at the bar in the Blue Beach. We could go talk to him now if you want."

"That would suit me fine." We walked together. "We

want to be cool with Miltos. This isn't an interrogation. We just want him to talk freely, and maybe we'll hear something useful, maybe some light will be shed."

Diogenes nodded. "Yeah, I'm with ya on that."

"Good. Then let's go see what Miltiades has to say. I didn't see him at the funeral, or after, did you?"

"No, but there were a lot of people, and I was pretty busy."

"Indeed you were. Pallbearing, having to discuss Pericles with every single person who knew him, bucking up the ones losing it. You performed admirably."

"Yeah, I guess."

The Blue Beach was a café/bar/restaurant next door to the Kronos grounds. It too was open-air, and we found Miltiades sitting at the bar. He was a wiry, dark guy in his mid-thirties, long dark hair loosely pulled back, sharp prominent nose, an attractive man. He had an Amstel in front of him. Diogenes sat down on the stool to his right, and I sat to Dio's right. Didn't want the man to feel hemmed in.

"Hey, Milto, what's going on?"

Miltiades turned a fairly neutral face to Diogenes and said, "The beer's cold and I'm drinking it." He nodded in my direction.

I ordered two Kaiser Pilsners from the bartender. Diogenes jumped right in. "Were you at the funeral?"

Miltiades shook his head. "Nah, I don't really do funerals. I hate the church, and let's face it, the dead don't care. He died, that's a fucking drag, but that's it. What do they say, 'Let the dead bury the dead.'"

Miltiades should have come down the beach with

the women, though it's not surprising that death was on everyone's mind.

Diogenes shook his head and asked, "What the fuck happened over there anyway?"

Miltiades shrugged. "I don't know. They found him naked in the walk-in, that's all I know."

I leaned forward and looked past Diogenes. "How was biz over there? Were they selling much food?"

He looked back at me. "It was steady, picking up I would say. I think August was going to be good."

"How do you know this?"

"I worked over there earlier this summer."

"Oh yeah. Did you quit?"

Miltiades stared at the wall behind the bar. "Let's just say we came to an agreement that I wouldn't work there anymore. I couldn't make it a couple or three times, you know, too much party, and it fucks up the schedule, someone has to cover for you, it was better for everyone. Anyway, I got a better gig, so it worked out."

"What's that?"

"I'm working for the municipality cleaning up the beach. It's fucking easy, and you can do it in any condition, you know what I mean." He finished his beer.

"You want another?"

"If you're buying, sure."

"The night Pericles died, did you see anything strange?"

He shook his head. "Nah. I was drinking here with Eleni. Then we went to Spider's and kept on. We got a pretty good buzz on till late. And then, bummer, Eleni had to go to work. Man, I couldn't have done it. I guess that's why I don't work there. And she finds Pericles chilled to death or something. She was feeling pretty rough to begin with, and she just puked right there in the sink after she saw him. Well duh, who wouldn't? Finding him there like that has really fucked her up big-time. It's gonna take a while to bring her around, you know what I'm saying?"

We sat on that one for a while. I turned to my right. From where I was seated there was a clear view through the vegetation to the front of the darkened Kronos campground restaurant.

Next morning I ran into Shrink Dogg on the beach. "Yo, Dogg, what's the word?"

He gave me a large smile. "Just had a marvelous swim, now I'm going for a coffee."

"Yeah, the water's great, isn't it? Hey, late afternoon I'm heading back to the mountain. Can I buy you lunch over at the Blue Beach before I go?"

"That'd be great. What time?"

"Two?"

"Meet you there."

When I got to the Blue Beach, Shrink Dogg was seated at the most exposed table in the place.

"Yo, Dogg. Hey, you mind if we sit over there?" I pointed to a table nearly obscured by palm fronds.

He laughed. "Feeling a little socially burned out by the events of the past days?"

"Something like that." We moved to my preferred table and settled our chairs in the sand.

We ordered wine and masses of food. I was ravenous and everything sounded good.

"So," he purred, "what conclusions have you come to concerning Pericles's sad demise?"

I paused for a minute. It sounded like he was parodying me. I drank some wine and took a deep breath. "First off, I have to swear you to secrecy. The same level of confidentiality as you have with your patients. I insist on that. What I'm going to say I haven't told Diogenes, 'cause let's face it, he can't keep a secret. But no one would benefit from this story getting out. And it is a story, an invention, something I've pieced together, and it might be completely erroneous, but I don't think so."

Shrink Dogg leaned forward in his chair conspiratorially. "Of course," he said under his breath, "nothing leaves this table. You have my word."

"Good. I trust you, man. I put it all together this morning, and I guess I need to run it by someone, just to confirm that I'm not completely out of it. There were several things about this event that didn't ring true. First, what the fuck is he doing in an unlocked, that's important, walk-in. No one kills themselves that way, and as everyone attested, including you, he wasn't depressed or suicidal. Fuck no, life was pretty good. It's summer in Greece on the beach for crying out loud. According the autopsy he hadn't taken any dangerous drugs or inadvertently mixed drugs and alcohol in some toxic combination. Once you've come to these conclusions, you must assume that he was locked in there deliberately by someone else. Are you with me so far?"

Shrink Dogg was intently focused. "Completely."

I took a breath and plunged on. "But who the fuck would do that to Pericles? He's the most popular guy on the beach. Beloved by all! I couldn't come up with anyone, I couldn't come up with a motive, so I tried to develop a motiveless murder narrative.

"I have an hypothesis. I have developed a story that makes sense to me. I don't have every detail nailed down, but I think something very similar occurred. Just as importantly, there's no proof. Absolutely nothing. I have no evidence, nor any way to get it. I can't interrogate anyone or look at phone records, get warrants, nor do I want to. I'm not a detective or whatever. I've never had a fantasy about being a cop." I laughed. "Hardly. And also, I realize that the narrative I'm about to lay out is the most positive spin possible given what we know.

"It's Wednesday midnight, and Miltiades and Eleni are here at the Blue Beach drinking at the bar. Something they do with great regularity. You know them both, right?"

"Yeah, we don't hang out, but yeah, I know them."

"Miltiades looks up and sees Pericles entering the closed restaurant for his nightly walk-through. He turns to Eleni and says, 'I want to talk to Pericles for a minute, I'll be right back.' Or, maybe he just says I gotta go talk to Yiorgos or some other area regular. Obviously, I don't know what he said to Eleni. He goes over to the closed restaurant. He can see that Pericles is now in the kitchen so he enters the dining room and peeks through the window of the kitchen door. Pericles is going through the kitchen checking that everything is sussed. Then he grabs the inventory clipboard, opens the walk-in door, and steps inside. At this moment Miltiades decides he's going to fuck with Pericles a bit, play a little prank. He enters the kitchen, and as he walks toward the refrigerator he grabs a meat thermometer from a little shelf over the ovens. He slams the walk-in door shut and sticks the meat thermometer in the locking mechanism. Pericles is shouting and banging on the door but you can't hear anything on the outside. He figures he'll leave him in there for a half hour or something, enough to freak him out a bit. He grabs a fifth of booze on the way out, he's no saint, and closes the door behind him.

"Back at bar he tells Eleni, 'I pulled a little trick on Pericles, I'll tell you later.' If he tells her right away, she'll race over and let him out, that's no fun. Let him chill for a while. They commence to drink. They pound it down. Don't forget, Miltos has a hot fifth with him. Then they get in his car and drive to Spider's, where they proceed to get roaring drunk, and Miltos forgets all about Pericles in the fridge. Eventually they get back to Eleni's place, where they have wild drunken sex, or they pass out. Either way, morning comes too soon. But not soon enough, you dig. The rooster crows, the alarm goes off, they wake up, and bang, Miltiades remembers Pericles! Oh fuck, screams Miltiades. Eleni, you have to get to Kronos! Of course I do, she says, I work today. You have to get there now! Pericles is locked in the walk-in! Imagine Eleni's face. It wouldn't look too good at the moment anyway, she's deeply hung over and has had about three hours of sleep. What are you fucking talking about? Miltiades gives her the short version. She screams and races out and jumps in Miltiades truck and puts the pedal to the metal. Ten minutes later she tears into the unlocked restaurant, the first one there for the first time ever, and yeah, the walk-in is locked. She extracts the thermometer and opens the door, and there's Pericles, naked and fetal and very dead. Oh fuck. She staggers out of the fridge. What now? I'm pretty sure that if you checked Eleni's phone records, the first call she makes that morning is to Miltiades. She wants to scream into the phone but probably whispers. By this time Miltiades has smoked a couple of cigs and downed a cup of coffee while he considers his situation. It's daytime, they can't dispose of the body. He tells her to ditch the thermometer but all she does is put it on a lower shelf. They agree on their story, which doesn't amount to any more than she came to work and found the boss in the fridge. She wipes down the door and handle of the fridge, of course, and decides to remove the inventory clipboard and hang it back where it lives. She doesn't do anything to the body, everyone has watched crime shows. I have no idea when she called the cops. If she calls them too early, it's suspicious. It's already suspicious that she's the first in, though nobody notices it. Maybe she waited for a while, which would have been difficult. But eventually she calls the cops."

Shrink Dogg rocked back in his chair and slowly clapped his hands. "Bravo man, that's a fantastic story. And very plausible, I think. How did you come up with it?"

"Just listening. Yesterday I heard two details that brought it together. One, Eleni is always late in the morning but this morning comes in early, we don't even know how early, even though she'd been out drinking till four or something, and second, she hangs with Miltiades, whom Pericles had fired only weeks ago. That and they were here, right in this bar only a few meters from the scene, the night of the big chill. As I said before, I couldn't figure out a motive, they don't strike me as homicidal, so I needed a story where they weren't. An accident. This narrative allows them to be the jolly sloppy losers they are."

"And you're not going to do anything with this?"

"No, I'm not. Pericles is dead, and nothing will bring him back. I don't have any evidence. Even if say the cops checked her phone's records, so what? She forgot her purse and called Miltiades to bring it, whatever. In the States, if they suspected her they might bring her in and scare her, make a deal so she could rat out Miltiades. That won't happen here. Ursula, the kids, the family, they're going to have to live with a mystery. And Miltiades and Eleni are going to have to live with murder, which Eleni appears to be having a hard time with. Nobody will live happily ever after. Except maybe Stein."

I grabbed a wee fish from the platter and held it up so she could see it. "Okay, it's the Canine Olympics. Representing Greece is Gertrude Stein. She catches this and she's into the finals. A hush settles over the crowd. And there's the toss. Stein leaps, she catches! She's into the finals! The crowd roars." Shrink Dogg and I made crowd noises.

8: Ragnar brings the world

Ragnar had the pong of doom about him, a sour scent of portent. He wasn't gloomy, though, just that the air around him wafted foreboding, determined disaster, of tragic outcomes still to be discovered. If you got to know him you quickly discovered that this was hardly the whole story, but there was no denying it. When he passed, sensitive people felt a shadow moving through the atmosphere, a specter that blocked the light. He used this aura of darkness to great effect. Few people took the time to know him well, he didn't invite intimacy. I was the rare one taken into his confidence. Mostly he was a connoisseur of chance and made his way leveraging his understandings on others' misconceptions of luck. Luck was the spark of existence, the galvanizing action that could be observed, gambled on, played out in every direction. It was an opportunity to improvise and test his ability to read the waves.

Gurdjieff clopped smartly up the hill, and I bounced along with him. With my bags strapped to his back there was still room enough for me. I'd been out of country for a while, touching base with old friends in London and in the States, and it was glorious to complete the last leg of the return trip on the back of Gurdjieff. When I was gone he stayed with people in the village. They were nice to him, but it wasn't the free life he lived at the hut. I took a cab from the bus station to where he was and loaded him up. He's always terribly frisky upon my returns.

The dogs stayed near the beach on a farm. The next day I could hear them as they hit the beginning of the trail, having leapt out of Mitso's truck before it even stopped. They caught the linger of Gurdjieff and my passing and sprinted up the path in full howl. I sat down in front of the hut, otherwise they'd knock me over. Sometime late in the afternoon Langston the crow put in an appearance and we were all together again.

It was a dry spring day, and I was airing out the hut. Everything was out hanging off trees and bushes or leaned up against the walls. Wildflowers insisted on my attention. I'd been gone a month, but in the hut it felt like a year. Suddenly the dogs made themselves scarce. I turned around and there was Ragnar, smiling, a walking stick in his hand, floppy hat on his head, a small pack on his back.

I jumped. "Rags! Where'd you come from?"

Ragnar laughed and pointed at me. "You're distracted, didn't even hear me coming. You're usually more alert. Maybe it's just getting old, huh?"

"Some of that, certainly. I depend on the dogs, but they're no good with you, are they?"

"No, they're not. When they feel my presence, or maybe it's just smell, they get out of the way, they make themselves scarce."

"Oh well, fuck it." We embraced. He felt thin beneath his jacket. We stepped back and held each other at arm's length. "Where have you been?"

He looked me in the eyes. His were dark indigo pools. He had a penetrating way about him, an intensity he could seemingly turn on and off, like a light switch. Only when he turned it on things got darker. Now they glazed and drifted lightly, and he said lazily, "The Black Sea. Varna, actually."

"What the fuck were you doing in Bulgaria?"

"Oh, you know, gambling."

I looked into his face but not particularly his eyes. There was a lot of story here. I nodded in anticipation. "Well you can tell me all about it. Coffee, tea, tsipuro?"

Ragnar grinned, shrugged off his pack and said, "Tsipuro would suit me fine."

I unfolded a couple of chairs and fetched the tsipuro, two glasses, and some olives from the hut. Ragnar was sprawled in a chair and the dogs were fanned out on the perimeter of the clearing. They were lying down and watching, fascinated and fearful. I poured us a drink. "Mazel tov." We clicked glasses.

"Last time you were here was what, two, three years ago?"

"Two and a half. You were still in the house."

"That's right, and you had been in . . ."

"Mexico, mostly, and then Prague just before here. But that's dull ancient history." He indicated the scene with a sweep of his arm. "I want to hear about this setup. What is this shit? You're a goddamn hermit now or something?

"Not hermit. Shaman."

Ragnar gagged on his tsipuro. "What the fuck are you talking about? Shaman? You're no more shaman than I'm a Cocker Spaniel." He laughed long and hard.

"See? It's working. You feel better already."

He wiped his eyes on his shirtsleeve. "Okay, I've recovered. Really, what is this shit all about?"

"Shaman is probably not the right word. Wise man on the hill, maybe holy fool, that's a better description."

Ragnar was grinning and nodding. "How does this scam work?"

"It's not a scam."

"What do you mean, it's not a scam! Gimme a break. You are not a fucking wise man. Come on, I've known you for far too many years to have to listen to this bullshit. What's the angle?"

"The angle, if you will, is to see if I can do it."

"Huh? That's it? Where does the wise guy part come in?"

"How it works is, people with problems or, I don't know, existential questions, come up the hill, and we hang out talking about it. I've got a sweat lodge over there, got some mushrooms and cannabis around. Often they spend the night, and then they leave."

"And this helps them?"

"I don't know. Maybe. Sometimes."

"And how much do they pay for this?"

"Nothing."

"What? You don't even charge them? That is *so* you." Ragnar leaned forward in his chair. "Let me get this straight. You moved out of your nice pad into this fucking hut where you wait for fucked-up people to come up here and lay their problems on you. And you don't charge so you can act without guilt." He leaned back. "That is some crazy shit, brother. I don't see what you're getting out of it."

"It's like theatre. Think of it as a performance piece."

He couldn't stop smiling. "Ah, a performance piece." He looked around. "Are you documenting? Have you got cameras in the trees?"

"Nah. I have no need to be accurate, so documentation is superfluous, redundant. I write some of it down, later, when I'm feeling inventive. I invent from what I hear.

Most of it never happened. We create a story, the visitors and I. I don't imagine your visit will rate a note."

"Is that so?" Ragnar turned to me and let loose with a deep chill stare. "Have I ever told you how tormented I am?"

"Often."

We remember differently. We'll agree precisely on a great deal of detail and action until suddenly our memories diverge sharply. We are both aware of this and find it utterly puzzling. And this occurs with events that only the two of us could remember, there being no others involved. It could be a primary fact, he went first or I did. Or something more subtle, a color, what music was playing, where we saw Luis Buñel's *Simon of the Desert*. Matters of interpretation were obvious and we ignored them, but sometimes we'd be caught up short, each of us simultaneously entertaining two thoughts: how could he remember it that way and am I wrong?

Am I wrong?" works as a mantra. It can paralyze as well. There are certain relationships where that friend of yours is trouble. Being their friend might be dangerous. And if you're lucky, you have other friendships where you are the risky one.

"So you suddenly leave Bulgaria and come here because you are missing me too much?"

"Exactly, my friend. Suddenly nothing else but your presence would do."

"And you had to leave town in a hurry?"

Ragnar laughed and shrugged. "Am I that predictable?"

"You do trouble too good, my man. What went down?"

"Oh, these rat-fucks tried to run a scam on me but I saw it coming from the opening contact. So I turned it on them. Suffice to say, they didn't see anything until their money was mine."

"And they were displeased."

"And then some. This is Varna, where nothing is on the up and up. It's crawling with every type of criminal you can imagine: thugs, con men, internet dark-market tech wizards, arms smugglers, sex traffickers, hit men, everybody's in the game."

"Sounds like your kind of scene."

"'Tis. I was thriving, mostly just playing cards. But when I flipped this stupid bullshit these punks were trying to run, they were exceedingly pissed. Violently so. No one is more outraged than a thief who's been ripped off."

"But you had an escape plan."

I got a benign look followed by, "It takes preparation to be in the game to this exalted age, hombre. I was convinced this would happen and disappeared moments after the play went down. They probably still think I'm in Varna. My hotel room is paid up. I've appointments for next week. I imagine it will take a few days before they realize I've flown."

"They can't trace you here?"

"How the fuck would they do that?"

"I don't know. That's your area of expertise. Can't they check flight manifests and that kind of shit?"

"Oh, I don't think it was that bad a beat that they'd expend big resources to catch me."

"How much?"

"Chump change. Two hundred large."

"They kill people for a lot less, don't they?"

"Of course they do. And the guys responsible for losing the dough have probably already been dealt with. You only lose that kinda money once. It's just that I don't believe the people further up the food chain are going to pursue the issue."

"Two hundred large is chump change?"

"The prosecutor hones in!" Ragnar laughed. "Okay, false bravado. It's a big score. But you need that kinda bankroll to stay in the game, in order to be able to play the hands that have to be played."

"You play in games that big?"

"Rarely. I'm mid-level and happy with it. But I want to play some bigger games too, and you have to have the bankroll. I'm also in that same range when it comes to the vaguely illegal. The bigger you are the more dangerous it gets. I'm the size that doesn't get pursued across international borders. Under the radar, as they say."

"You hope."

Ragnar Miguel Lopez was the dazzling product of a Mexican father and a Danish mother, with dark skin, long dirty blond hair, strong indigenous facial features, tall and thin with indigo eyes burning out. This, coupled with a fluid, lively intelligence and curiosity, made him irresistible to women. He had spent extended periods of time in both countries, but we met in California while attending university in San Francisco. We fancied ourselves poet-artists and dashed about town performing poetically, or so we thought. What was sure was that we sparked each other, complimented and deciphered the world in remarkably similar fashion but from different angles. Our vision overlapped at many points, and together we could

151

observe the world with a vividness that was addictive. It was a magnetic thing; I played positive to his negative, both of us too much of what we brought to the table. Our relationship leavened it out a bit though many found that together we were almost intolerable with constant inside jokes and obscure references, some of which we made up, of course. We loved to write poems together, sometimes for two voices, sometimes one, and then perform them on the bus or street corner. Later we graduated to bars, cafés, galleries. Even the odd university. We were the new for a few minutes.

"So do the pilgrims make appointments or what?" Ragnar spoke from the hammock.

I was stirring stew for supper. "Nah, it's all open. Whoever wants to walk up the mountain."

"And you think that by keeping it all loose and free-form you're presenting a . . . what, anarchist vision? The spontaneous madman spouting truths, that sort of thing?"

Old friends aren't supposed to cut you any slack, that's the rules. "I don't know, something like that, I suppose."

"What nonsense!"

"But the step-up is a big part of it, just like a con or a magic trick. They've exhausted other avenues of query, or they don't trust the regular methods. They're ready when they get here."

"For what? The whole shebang is too romantic. Hermits, holy fools, it's like Dostoevsky or something. It's the fucking twenty-first century, man. You're not pushing against the setup hard enough. Though I know what you're doing. It's obvious."

"Yeah, what?"

"You're sucking stories, man. Folks come up here and gush out their tragedies, suicides and tumors, rejections and hates. And you sitting there by the fire nodding, all wise, but thinking, hmm, that's a good one. And then you change the names or tweak 'em a bit and voilà, original material!"

Like I said, everyone needs someone like this, but you don't want them around too much. Neighbors, for instance, wouldn't work. "Sure, that's how they pay, if you want. But I give 'em something back."

"It's not bold enough, it's practically nostalgic. Here's what I did in Spain a year ago. It's similar in nature but right in the belly of the beast. I'm in Granada, and I'm wandering through this cathedral, getting out of the sun, checking out the stained glass and statuary. And there's a confessional booth right there, and one of the faithful is just leaving—heading up to the altar to say their ten Hail Marys and five Our Fathers for fucking the neighbor's sheep. Thou shalt not covet thy neighbor's lamb. Moments later a young priest exits from God's side of the booth. He throws a little switch which turns out the light above the confessional. Nobody in. He walks off, and before I can think it through, I jump in the priest's nook, pull the curtain, and hit the light. God is fucking in, mofos! Bring on the sin! So I sit in there for fifteen minutes or so, I'm about to give it up, when in steps a guilty one."

I'm laughing by now. "That is great. So what happened?"

"So this person, I'm guessing forty-year-old woman, middle-class, mumbles the preamble, and I bless her and ask what are your sins, my child. I'm expecting bullshit like I took the Lord's name in vain or thought evil thoughts and the like, but no, it takes her a while to get around to it, but it turns out she's fucking her brother-in-law! Biblical, muthafucka, Old Testament rutting. So I ask her, this is all in Spanish, of course, I ask her whether she enjoys this. She sez something like it's all she can think about. So I quiz her on the details. How many times, where, anything special about this boinking, and she just chatters away. Obviously she's been desperate to confess. She can't keep it to herself any longer! She digs this guy. He's really lighting her up."

"Fantastic. So what did you tell her?"

"Aha, you'll like this. I realized I had a certain moral dilemma here. So while I hate the fucking church and the whole idea of God, this woman is in need. She's come seeking solace or comfort or condemnation. Who the fuck knows, but I realize I can't just blow her off, though I'm tempted. But if God rejects her she might leave the church and throw herself under a bus or something. She's in a really tough situation, so I decide to help her out."

"Beneath the Mephitic demeanor beats some organ of compassion."

"Hold the canonization, you haven't heard my help."

"Something tells me penance ain't part of it."

"You're catching up. So I get all the details. She's been married for twenty-odd years, has three kids, youngest is seventeen. She works at home doing what sounded like high-end tailoring while the hubby works for a company that buys and markets agricultural products. Food production is huge in Spain. Anyway, he's middle management, working his way up, consequently putting in a lot of hours and leaving ole Maria, of course I don't know her name, far too much alone. In the last couple of years she's been having it off with his brother. First it was on rare occasion but now she's getting that good thing at least once a week. Typically, she doesn't want to divorce her husband, she likes the stability, hell, she likes him, and, this is Catholic Spain, the shame of adultery, no way is she going that route. So I try and help her out by tightening up her game a bit. You know, some subterfuge techniques."

"Of which you are an acknowledged master."

Ragnar nodded. "First, I told her to never use the phone. Don't get an extra one either. They're like time bombs. Sometime somebody finds it and then you're fucked. I told her to open an anonymous email account and to use it sparingly. The less media usage the better. And she doesn't fuck him in her apartment, no way, someone will eventually see him coming or going and even though he's the brother-in-law it won't look good. From now on, on assignation day she's going to walk about ten minutes away from her apartment and then discreetly take a cab to a variety of small hotels on the outskirts of town, none of them anywhere near her husband's place of work, of course. She can incorporate delivery of work in this. Ideally the brother would rent an apartment, and I suggested that, but that sounded too permanent or something. For twenty minutes we discussed how she could successfully cheat on her husband with his brother. And I told her, you can't ignore your husband, the household has got to be happy too, it's gonna be tough keeping all these balls in the air, or in your hand, but I assured her she was up to the task."

"And she thought you were a priest this whole time?"

"Yeah, I wondered about that too. I only had her voice to go by, what with the screen thing between us, but as far as I could tell, she was so desperate for a helping hand that she dropped all suspicion. I told her she was a servant of love and that god was looking down with approval at how she was spreading it around. And when I was trying to dismiss her she asked, but Father, what about penance? And I told her, your love is no sin, my child. You are doing god's work. If you're feeling a little guilty, give something to the poor. And off she went. I peeked out but she was walking away, wearing a coat, hair looked nice. And then I got the fuck out of there before some other sinner wanted to unload."

"Damn, that is good. Bravo." I applauded. "And okay, I'll admit it, that's better than what I'm doing here. More spontaneous, darker and more dangerous, with your usual wicked wit. 'Share your love with the world, girl.' But you see, my setup works too. Look at the great story you brought me."

Ragnar bowed his head. "I endeavor to give satisfaction."

Langston dropped down and landed on the table. Ragnar held out a small bit of bread, and he took it and lifted off. As opposed to the dogs, Langston rather liked Rags's vibe.

Evening came on and we built a fire in the pit against the chill. We were back to sipping tsipuro, but slowly, as the night gave every intention of stretching out like a long dog after a nap. Rags seemed relieved to be able to talk about things outside his life as a card shark/con man. He put his feet up near the fire. "Okay, I'll grant you, this is pretty nice. Look, even the dogs are relaxing." And they were, the lure of the fire bringing them in, in spite of their reservations. Owls seeking mates called through the trees.

"Rags, how's Luciana?"

"She's studying physics in Barcelona."

"Hard-science woman. Do you think she'll move back to Mexico?"

"Oh yeah. That's what she claims, anyway. But, you know, maybe she'll meet somebody or get a really good job. We'll see when she graduates."

"You mean she hasn't got a guy? I find that hard to believe."

"Of course she has a guy. She's got lotsa guys. She just hasn't met the special one."

"The *especial hombre* can be hard to find."

"No more than the *especial mujer*."

"*Es verdad, mi hermano*. And here, fireside, is living proof."

Ragnar held his hands to the fire. "How did we end up here in the mountains, alone and in the dark?"

"Because we can't resist the goof, the spoof, the cosmic joke."

"Which is just another way of saying we aren't inclined to take life seriously."

"Is that it? Life must be drama and not comedy? Since when? Does serious really trump hilarious? For instance, your confession bit in Spain. Are the folks who come in with the recorded tour playing in their ears, snapping photos of every bit of fresco and statuary, really experiencing the cathedral or just doing what they're supposed to do? Whereas you, playing the priest, are rubbing up against the faithful struggling with desire and treachery. You're doing what you're absolutely not supposed to do. It's like Ginsberg said, the work of life is to ease the pain of living. What better way than with a laugh? What the fuck?"

"But the woman in the confessional wasn't laughing. We're cowards. Neither of us had the courage to do stand-up comedy."

"Look ma, no *cojones*."

"Performance art, poetry readings, they're not the same thing. There, silence is often the best response. But with comedy, if nobody laughs you're dead."

"That's not funny. Off with his head!"

"Is the court jester ever well-fed?"

"It has to do with what he said."

"Rule of thumb: no yucks, no bread."

"And by their noses they are led."

"Dumb, luckless, and full of dread."

"Should we leave it at that? I've lost the thread."

"What? A little slow this evening? You used to keep it going till their ears bled."

"That's what she said, and then we wed."

"Was that the inbred coed?"

I burst out laughing at that point, which meant I lost and had to fetch more of what we were drinking. That was our rule developed back when we thought we were funny. "Okay, okay, you win, though she gave great head."

"Too late, muthafucka. There's nothing lamer than after-the-fact humor."

"How true. I bow to your superior wit, '*il miglior fabbro*,' as Eliot put it."

"No wonder we're alone and in the dark."

How's the international poker world these days?" I brought another jug of wine to the fire.

"Fiercely competitive. Everyone can play. Thousands and thousands of them. So it often boils down to stamina and nerve. There are hundreds of terrific Asian players, mostly Chinese, who play what appears to be a wild, reckless style, but it isn't. I find them very difficult to read. And reading players is my thing."

"What? You mean they're inscrutable?"

Ragnar laughed. "Yeah, that sounds really stupid, doesn't it? Like fucking Fu Manchu. Ah, round eye, you think I am bluffing but I have the nuts. Call me and find out."

"Do you think Chinese people are as bad at doing impersonations of us as we are of them?"

"Oh, just as bad, I'm sure, but that's the thing, ethnic impressions are for your group, so they only have to be funny, not accurate. I mean within this context. We left stand-up comedy behind, or we never caught up to it. But really, what do you mean, 'us'?"

"Aha, the Viking Aztec speaks. I don't know how I'd begin to impersonate you. It feels an impossible task. But you must be burned out by the poker playing, not to mention the odd hustle or scam. I mean, everybody's younger than you, right?"

"Way. I am fried, done. I'm thinking I won't go back to it."

"Does this have anything to do with the two hundred large beat you put on those guys?"

"Partially. But there are places to play all over the world, so those guys wouldn't be hard to avoid. No, I just can't do it anymore. I'm thinking I'll just stay in one place. You know, fuck it, I'm out of the game."

"But where? And what are you going to do? Have you got enough stashed away?"

"I've got a decent stash but not to live here, in Europe or in the States. So Mexico it is. It's not a consolation choice, you know. Even if I had a much larger bankroll

I would still return to Mexico. It's the most comfortable place for me, especially if Luciana moves back."

"And do what? You're a guy who has always needed action." I could hardly believe it.

"*Nada mas.* Worn out, enough already."

"Wow. This feels momentous. I'm afraid I don't have any champagne."

Ragnar laughed derisively. "Yeah, right. What's to celebrate? Look at us. Two guys in their mid-fifties sitting on a mountain. No women. No gigs. Children far away. A pretend shaman and a gambler on the run."

"Sounds like a Willie Nelson song."

Ragnar lazily raised his palm. We high-fived.

"I guess I better break out the cannabis."

"Might as well."

The next two days meandered by as we luxuriated in each others' company. We took my small library of poetry out of the hut, stacked it on the table, and while drinking tea, read through the stack, Ragnar in the hammock, myself at the table. Once in a while one of us would read a poem or a section of a poem out loud. From the hammock Ragnar announced:

> *I have had to learn the simplest things*
> *last. Which made for difficulties.*
> *Even at sea I was slow, to get the hand out, or to cross*
> *a wet deck.*
>
>   *The sea was not, finally, my trade.*
> *But even my trade, at it, I stood estranged*
> *from that which was most familiar. Was delayed,*
> *and not content with the man's argument*

that such postponement
is now the nature of
obedience
> *that we are all late*
> *in a slow time,*
> *that we grow up many*
> *And the single*
> *is not easily*
> *known*

"Yeah, Olson is always pertinent when you are doing nothing. It's as though you struggle with him as he staggers down the page. Okay, here's a bit from another 'how the hell did I get here' poem.

> *My mother would be a falconress,*
> *and I her gerfalcon, raised at her will,*
> *from her wrist sent flying, as if I were her own*
> *pride, as if her pride*
> *knew no limits, as if her mind*
> *sought in me flight beyond the horizon.*
>
> *Ah, but high, high in the air I flew.*
> *And far, far beyond the curb of her will,*
> *were the blue hills where the falcons nest.*
> *And then I saw west to the dying sun—*
> *it seemed my human soul went down in flames.*

"I know that poem. It's a . . . damn, I can't conjure up the name."

"Robert Duncan."

"Shit yes, of course. Okay, this one could almost have

been written here."

> *Down valley a smoke haze*
> *Three days heat, after five days rain*
> *Pitch glows on the pine cones*
> *Across the rocks and meadows*
> *Swarms of new flies.*
>
> *I cannot remember things I once read*
> *A few friends, but they are in cities.*
> *Drinking cold snow-water from a tin cup*
> *Looking down for miles*
> *Through high still air.*

"'Sourdough Mountain Lookout.' I love the early Snyder stuff. The Han Shan/Li Po influence makes them buoyant rather than heavy. Here's another country poem.

SHEEP IN FOG

> *The hills step off into whiteness.*
> *People or stars*
> *Regard me sadly, I disappoint them.*
>
> *The trains leave a line of breath.*
> *O slow*
> *Horse the color of rust,*
>
> *Hooves, dolorous bells—*
> *All morning the*
> *Morning has been blackening,*
> *A flower left out.*

My bones hold a stillness, the far
Fields melt my heart.

They threaten
To let me through to a heaven
Starless and fatherless, a dark water."

"Nice, but I haven't a clue."

"Sylvia Plath."

"Huh? Never read it. It would be better, I think, to not know anything about the lives of the poets. Her biography changes everything. Maybe all poems should be presented anonymously?"

"Okay," I said, "here's one that you can dig anonymously, but knowing the context gives it a more piquant flavor, shall we say. I'll even give you the title."

PHONE CALL TO RUTHERFORD

"It would be—
         a mercy if
you did not come see me…

"I have dif-fi / culty
         speak-ing. I
cannot count on it, I
am afraid it would be too em-
         ba
         rass-ing
for me ."

              —Bill, can you still

answer letters?

"No . my hands
are tongue-tied . You have…made

a record in my heart.
             Goodbye."

"Oh, that's very nice, 'my hands are tongue-tied,' 'a record in my heart,' beautiful. Now give the biographical punch-line."

"It's Paul Blackburn, a fave of mine, writing about talking on the phone to the stroke- and depression-debilitated William Carlos Williams, who lived in Rutherford, New Jersey. Blackburn was especially nimble with regards to the geography of the page, you know, open field composition, as Olson and Creeley put it. In this poem he does really exquisite, finely detailed work to render Williams's broken language with spacing and odd punctuation so that you know the stuttering, mind-gagging speech. His technique tells you just how to read it."

Ragnar peeked over the top of the hammock. "You're a fucking poet, man. Why are you pretending to be a fucking shaman? I do have a fragment of Williams lodged in my memory."

> *It is difficult*
> *to get the news from poems*
>   *yet men die miserably every day*
>   *for lack*
> *of what is found there.*

"Good one, Rags. Memory still functioning. 'As

essential as bread' is how Milosz put it."

"Yeah, that's the romantic view, but if I ever show up at your door hungry, don't give me poetry. Fettucini carbonara would be nice. Or some lamb on the grill. A good wine. Then we could read poetry, but on a full stomach."

"I will bear that in mind when hungry you knock upon my door. Let poetry be dessert. All right, let me read you one you won't know. Even has a poker theme. It's from a series of poems, many of which have these blitzy, fabulous titles which sort of echo the titles of Tang dynasty poets but are utterly original, as is the poet.

RUNNING YOUR HAND OVER IT TO CALCULATE ITS DIMENSIONS YOU THINK AT FIRST IT IS STONE THEN INK OR BLACK WATER WHERE THE HAND SINKS IN THEN A BOWL OF ELSEWHERE FROM WHICH YOU PULL OUT NO HAND

Today I have not won. But who can tell if I shall win tomorrow.
So he would say to himself going down the stairs.
Then he won.

Good thing because in the smoke of the room he found himself wagering
his grandfather's farm (which he did not own)
and forty thousand dollars cash (which he did).

Oh to tell her at once he went slapping down the sidewalk
to the nearest phone booth, 5 a.m. rain pelting his neck.

Her voice sounded broken into. Where were you last night.
Dread slits his breath.
Oh no

he can hear her choosing another arrow now from the little
quiver
and anger goes straight up like trees in her voice holding
his heart tall.

I only feel clean he says suddenly when I wake up with you.
The seduction of force is from below.
With one finger

the king of hell is writing her initials on the glass like
scalded things.
So in travail a husband's
legend glows, sings.

"Jesus Christ, that's great! What, who?"

"Anne Carson, Canadian poet about our age. A classicist. She's often really really good. That's from a book called *The Beauty of the Husband*.

"Throw that text over here. I want more."

I tossed the book and Ragnar snatched it out of the air. At that moment the dogs exploded into barks and raced down the trail toward the road. We listened to them take their collective roar through the woods. They sounded aggressive. Ragnar was already out of the hammock.

"How long till whoever that is gets here?"

"Two or three minutes. Why?"

Suddenly dead-serious, Ragnar gathered up the books

and carried them to the hut and came back out with his backpack. I was out of my chair but unsure what was happening.

"Max. I think we should make ourselves scarce. Immediately."

"Fuck, you think it's the Bulgarians?"

He winced. "Possibly."

"Follow me."

We made our way up the hill behind the hut to a dense thicket of holm oak where you could see below while being completely hidden. The dogs were furiously barking. Gurdjieff didn't like the sound of it and pushed off into the bush. We were breathing hard and on our knees peering through the holly-like leaves of the oak. Ragnar put his hand on my shoulder. "I'm sorry, man. I didn't believe they'd pursue it. I still can't figure out how they traced me here. If, that is, that's them coming up the trail."

"Damn, Rags, you really think they've found you? I mean, I don't like the sound of the dogs, but how is it possible?"

"Like I said, I can hardly get my mind around it."

We watched and listened as the barking drew near. I was stunned with this sharp acceleration from poetry to a dire situation that didn't bode well. That was fucking dangerous, goddamn it. The dogs entered the clearing before the hut still raising a mighty ruckus. They were followed by two men who looked direct from central casting. Burly men in their thirties, jackets and jeans and sport shoes, hair sheared short above their hard Slavic faces, they alertly scanned the scene while producing revolvers. We unconsciously held our breaths. I was trembling.

One of the men walked into the hut while the other checked the shed. Ragnar and I both noticed the teacup that was still on the table outside. There was another on the ground by the hammock. They wouldn't need to be geniuses to figure two people had just left. Having found nothing, they stood before the hut and scanned the woods on the hill above. The dogs were still barking furiously. We crouched even lower but could still see clearly. One of the men aimed his gun at Voltaire and fired. The dog dropped to the ground. It was breathtaking, like a punch to the stomach.

"Aw fuck," I whispered, "he shot Voltaire."

Bukowski snarled and growled at the man, who then shot him too. He flipped backward on to his back and was still. The other three dogs ran into the bushes in fear. Good dogs. If I had been down there they would have stayed till the last one fell. I was weeping now, my body convulsing, and Ragnar had his arms around me and was whispering into my ear. "I'm so sorry, brother. I know they're family." Through it all we didn't once take our eyes off the drama playing out below us.

The other man, who hadn't discharged his weapon yet, walked back into the hut. He exited a couple of minutes later, and pretty soon smoke was billowing out of the door and windows of the hut. It felt like a limb was being torn off, an emotional appendage ripped from my life. The dogs, the hut, they were bringing down the curtain on this show. Because they were dissatisfied, because they felt they were owed, and what they wanted was both close and far away, they aimed to violate. They stomped around the clearing for ten minutes or so while the hut burned, looking for something else, but realized they wouldn't have any luck pursuing us through the wild. Maybe they even suspected we were watching them? It probably drove them nuts.

The men spent another twenty minutes watching the hut burn; it wasn't really taking off but smoldering and generating a lot of smoke. They sat in the chairs at the table and stared intensely at the hillside behind the hut, often at the spot where we were hidden. We didn't move. We tried to slow our breathing to a meditative state. I was thinking of the dogs, their joyous loyalty, how they functioned as a pack, and I thought of all the people I had met just being in that hut, folks from all over the world taking the time to hike up the mountain and tell me their story, often in a very naked fashion, telling me things they'd never uttered to another person. It was a very privileged perch, and now the world was saying it was time to climb down.

Ragnar was profoundly still, yet looking at his profile, a few centimeters away, it seemed I could see his brain working, plotting, considering. Was he thinking of revenge? He wasn't a violent man but was comfortable functioning in a violent world. He expected it, which probably saved us. Even swooning over the poetry of Anne Carson, his antenna was alert. It was part of our history, Ragnar getting us in and out of trouble. But we weren't out of this yet, not by a long shot.

Then the men with guns gave up their vigil. They hadn't flushed us out. One of them kicked over the table and the other looked around for something to shoot, but the dogs were lying low and Gurdjieff was nowhere to be seen. They walked off down the trail toward the road, and we started breathing normally. It felt like the birds began to sing, though more likely we started hearing them again.

We began to talk, but in whispers.

"Those were the guys, right?"

Ragnar nodded, still sorting it all in his head.

I was in the dark and asked, "So, what's our plan now?"

"Extreme caution is the order of the day."

I snorted with derision. "Yeah, I got that. By the looks of it, I would think they'd kill us without giving it a thought."

"More than likely, but they won't kill us without at least trying to get their money back."

"Where is the money, if you don't mind my asking?"

"Bitcoins. Impossible for them to get their hands on it."

"Which means?"

"They'll kill us if they catch us."

I let out a breath of air. "Jesus Christ, Rags, what the fuck are we going to do now?" I pulled my hand through my hair and stretched out a leg. "Okay, I have great respect for your abilities, your improvisations, your confidence, but are you telling me this could be the last day of our lives?"

"That's always a possibility. I'll bet you've told some of your pilgrims that very thing."

"Yeah, but this is a bit more vivid, you know what I mean?"

"Right. Okay, let's begin now. I think we should stay hidden until dark. They might have walked just a brief way down the trail and circled back, to see if we emerge. That's what I would do. They're probably convinced that they're just behind me."

"Which they are."

"And they have no other option but to keep looking for me in this area. I think they'll keep snooping around waiting for me to resurface. That means we have to make our escape though the mountains."

I sighed. "It is 'we,' isn't it?"

"Obviously. They have done their homework and know all about you. You're the only link they have. Before we go any further, let me say how sorry I am about the whole damn thing. I was sure they wouldn't find me. In retrospect I should have taken a longer, more circuitous route. You know, gone to Italy, meandered a bit, taken the ferry to Greece from Brindisi. Lingered in Patras. That sort of thing."

"Hindsight means you're looking at the past through your asshole."

Ragnar stifled a laugh. "Okay, let's be still and see if we hear or see anything. I'm getting the sense these guys aren't as lame as I took them to be."

We waited as the day waned. We were on the east side of the Tayegetos Mountains, so sunset came early. A half-hour into the wait Stein found us but was happy just to lie next to us while I stroked her. I wasn't concerned with the other dogs, O'Keeffe and Derrida. They would appear as soon as I whistled for them. Gurdjieff hadn't gone far, I was sure of that. They were all still my responsibility, and any escape plan we made had to include them. On the other hand, making our way through the mountains on foot would suit them just fine.

The seconds of our lives ticked away, as they have a habit of doing. Finally it was dark, we hadn't heard or seen anything since the dog murderers had left, at least two hours, and we made our way down through the forest using light from Ragnar's phone.

I crouched by both the dogs. It had appeared from up above that they died instantly, we hadn't observed any movement, and certainly there was no sign of life now. Poor bastards. Their devotion to the turf but essentially to me had led to their demise. I placed my hands on them and wept again. "The weight of the world is love," as the poet put it. Life is an accumulation of burdens, and then at some point you begin shedding them because you can't remember why you were carrying them, or even what they are. That's the promised reward of demented old age, and a lie most likely. That these beasts met a swift, violent death in service to me took away for a moment my fear, bordering on terror, of what these Bulgarian gangsters might do to us if they caught us, and in its stead I thought of the loyalty dogs have to offer, an emotional attachment that humans are incapable of, except, sometimes, a parent with a child. That's what we hope, anyway. All manner of curious things can happen if you feed a creature and treat it well. I looked up at Ragnar and said, "I don't know if I should do something, bury them or I don't know."

Ragnar was standing above me aiming his phone light down on Voltaire. He gripped me by the shoulder. "Maybe you should leave them where they are. Those fuckers might come back tomorrow, and if you've moved the corpses they'll know for sure that you, and possibly me, are around."

I stood up, and Ragnar turned off the light to save the batteries. It was very dark, and it took a minute or so for my eyes to adjust. It was like speaking in the void. "Don't you think they know we were here?"

"Probably. But if they return tomorrow and find the dogs moved, buried, whatever, they'll know we are very close at hand, that we haven't gotten very far away, and they'll intensify their search."

"I suppose if they've tracked you this far they're not going to give up easily." I'm not someone who wants to treat dogs like humans. And I don't really care much what happens to the dead, because I'm pretty convinced that nothing does. So burials and the like don't motivate me. Within hours, maybe already, a great variety of beings will begin to feed on these dogs, and within a couple of weeks all that will be left is fur and bones, and the fur will blow away and dust will cover the bones. "All right. I get it. This way they won't know how much of a head start we have. And the less they know the better, I guess. I mean, I've never been pursued with murderous intent. I don't like the feeling. It's scary shit, Rags. I've lived my life in such a way that this sort of thing wouldn't possibly happen, for fuck sake." I was shaking.

Ragnar exhaled noisily. "Okay, I'm going to say I am powerfully sorry about this mess I've brought to your holy-man scene. It's a colossal fuck-up. But I don't want to keep saying 'I'm sorry.' So take this profound apology that I make with full sincerity, and from now on let's focus on putting distance between those guys and us."

"Staying alive."

"That's the idea. So put on your dancing shoes. This is your territory so you have to get us out of here."

"Jesus fucking Christ."

Everything was ruined in the hut. For the flames' inauguration they'd fashioned a pyre of poetry. I grabbed a thermos and a knife. They hadn't touched the shed, and I found a small tent and a couple of crappy sleeping bags that someone had left behind. I can't remember, did I drive them away with some cockeyed advice? I hauled

Gurdjieff's saddle out and softly called for him. He arrived a minute later along with O'Keeffe and Derrida. They immediately went and sniffed their fallen comrades, the pack diminished. We filled some plastic water bottles from the tank, grabbed a sack of dog food (their grub was in the shed, lucky bastards) and a few apples. Not much. We tied it to the donkey's saddle.

I took another look around, couldn't see much of anything. "Okay, beasts, we're clearing out and we may never be back. It was a curious time, while it lasted." I slapped Gurjieff on the hindquarters, and we began to slowly make our way, stumbling in the dark up the mountainside.

We spent the night beneath a rock outcropping, not bothering with the tent. It wasn't a true three-dog night, but having lost their discomfort with Ragnar, they slept up close and kept us warm. I awoke minutes before sunrise came over the Parnonas across the valley. The birds were tweeting and trilling. Ragnar was already up, sitting in a squat like a Kabul merchant and smoking a cigarette. I sat down next to him.

"I didn't know you stilled smoked?"

"I don't." He offered me a drag, I declined, and the coming sun was a liquid light, the range ridge molten, and then a thin apricot ray fanned out over the mountains, followed ever so slowly by a swelling, blinding light that briefly strobed before filling itself in. "You sleep any?"

"Not much."

I had spent much of the night considering our options. "Okay, here's what I'm thinking. We can't go east, down. That's where they are. Fortunately, we are the needle in the haystack. They can't possibly take into account all the alternative routes we can use or places where we can come down off the mountain. We have two choices. North would involve less walking, I believe. We'd cross a ridge up here and make our way in a northwest direction. We can hit this small settlement at the pass, or we could head further west and come down into Artemesia, where you could catch a bus to Kalamata. Maybe even a cab right to the airport. You'd be exposed in Artemesia while waiting for a bus. I know a family from Artemesia, but the member I know won't be there, so it doesn't count as a resource."

"Yeah, but what about you?"

"After you get gone I might head south. I've got people south of here near Arna. It's several days' walk. There's space for Gurdjieff and the dogs, and I can lie low for a couple of weeks or whatever. If you want to go south from here with me, you can eventually cut over to West Mani and down to the sea, where you can catch a cab in Kardamyli to the Kalamata airport. The only danger lies in that last stretch of getting to the airport. That's when you'll be publicly exposed. But up here in the mountains they can't find us."

Ragnar was slowly beating a stick against a rock while the sun lifted off the Parnonas. "Then south it is. Let's stay together as long as we can. Going south, isn't that what we're doing, metaphorically?" He paused and watched the sun. "What are we going to eat?"

"Fucking tree bark and raw tubers, dude. We're gonna be hunter fucking gatherers. Get in touch with your Neanderthal roots. Fuck. I agree, no more 'I'm sorrys,' but that doesn't negate the undeniable fact that you are the cause of this great cock-up. Nevertheless, I intend to eat, so I'll use your phone to call a friend down in the valley who can bring up supplies to a rendezvous somewhere around Anavryti. He'll love the whole subterfuge, the drama of it."

"The danger rush." Ragnar stood up. "Earlier the better, I should think."

"Let's do it. Come on, dogs, Gurdjieff, we're hitting the trail."

Beneath a clear, hard blue sky we climbed through the woods until we reached the tree line. Far below, Lakonia stretched out before us, Sparti a white sprawl amidst orchards of olive and orange. Crocuses burst from smudges of dirt between the rocks. The Lakonian Gulf was visible far to the south. I pointed north to a ridge between two peaks. "That's where Briseis's ashes are, or were. Now they're just part of the mountain."

"I've never seen it from this angle."

"Yeah. Of course you haven't." I couldn't quite make out the stupa Yiorgos and I had built so long ago. "'What thou lovest well remains, the rest is dross.'"

"The rest is dross. Ezra Pound provides the emergency language. We are out of fuel and there isn't any flat place to put it down. The pilot is so very sorry."

"And there are no refunds in heaven. Discard your coupons at the gate."

We stood a long while looking, hearing the air faintly whistle about us, the sun's heat building. We heard a raptor cry and turned to the west, where a motionless eagle was rising on a thermal column. As it came level with us, it twitched some feathers and soared off to the south. When it wasn't visible anymore, Ragnar said, "I propose we follow that bird."

We found the E4, the European hiking trail, and our

curious caravan, with Stein leading the way, followed by Ragnar and Derrida, Gurdjieff and myself, Langston above us, and O'Keeffe trailing behind, made our careful way south.

At noon I called my friend Yiorgos, gave him the situation, and told him what we needed. He thought he could gather the kit and food and meet us in the late afternoon in Anavryti. Three hours later I pointed to a small monastery below us. "Anavryti is just four kilometers from that. Yiorgos is going to do a bit of a reccie about the village first, just to make sure your Bulgarians aren't hanging out sipping tsipuro."

"How likely is that?"

"I don't know, but let Yiorgos play spy. If you look at a map, which we can assume our pursuers have, and you make a lucky guess as to our escape route, then Anavryti would be a place you might go and linger for a while."

"Then why are we rendezvousing there?"

"Access. There are very few roads that come up this high. Yiorgos is driving up with his van. But he's a country man, he won't attract any attention. After he's cased the village, take ten minutes max, he'll call us and we'll fine-tune our rendezvous."

With a smile Ragnar said, "All right. See, you *are* cut out for this sort of thing."

"No I'm not. So forget it. I'm not playing Robert Redford to your Paul Newman."

Ragnar whistled a chorus of "Raindrops keep falling on my head."

An hour later we were hidden in the trees above the monastery. The dogs were snoozing, Gurdjieff was grazing as best he could, and our stomachs were grumbling.

"What's your friend bringing?"

"Two plastic five-liter bottles of water, a little petro gas cooker so we can make tea, several bags of paxamadi, a couple of salamis, some dried fruit, figs, apricots, some nuts, a chunk of feta, some olives."

Ragnar slapped his hands together. "Really? He's bringing all that? Fantastic! I can't wait."

"It shouldn't be long."

The phone rang. Ragnar took a glance and handed it to me.

"Yiorgo, where are you?"

"I'm driving toward the monastery. I think I saw your guys. They were sitting at that café in the village, the one by the spring."

"You're shitting me. Describe them."

"I don't need to. I'm sending you a photo that I discreetly took."

I turned to Ragnar. "Yiorgos thinks our guys are in Anavryti. He's sending a photo." We sat staring at the phone, waiting for the bad news. Sure enough, there they were, smoking and sipping coffee. "What the fuck."

Ragnar snatched the phone from me and asked, "Yiorgos, this is Ragnar. Did they notice you?"

"No way. I parked my van and went into the café and bought a to-go coffee, and while I was waiting for it I snapped off the shot. They were sitting outside watching the village. They didn't see a thing."

"Is anyone following you?"

"I'm looking in the mirror right now, there's nothing but dust behind me."

"Okay. We're being extra cautious here for good reason.

These men are capable of murder. It's not a TV show. Why don't you stop at the monastery, get out, drink your coffee, have a smoke, and wait. We'll be able to see you. After half an hour call us back, and we'll organize where we'll meet."

"Wow. Do you really think all that's necessary?"

"Absolutely."

From our position above we watched Yiorgos drive up and park outside the monastery. He got out and walked to a bench that provided a view of the valley below and proceeded to drink his coffee.

"Damn, Rags, you really underestimated these guys."

"That is exceedingly apparent. They've proven themselves to be quite adept and tenacious, which is unfortunate, especially as they have one great advantage."

"What's that?"

"They are hard men willing to use violence, whereas we have been softened by our bourgeois life in the West, and the violence has been blanched out of us. We don't have the hunger or the will for it. Which is why we run and they pursue. If they thought we were capable of responding with violent force, they would be far more cautious. As it is, they're fearless."

I sighed. "All true, but you're failing to mention a key element in our conundrum."

"Pray tell."

"You have their motherfucking money, and if you didn't we wouldn't be on the run. Two hundred fucking large, man. How long does it take to come up with that kinda scratch in Bulgaria?"

Ragnar nodded his head and watched Yiorgos light a cigarette. "A lifetime. But you don't have to go on and on about it."

"Excuse me. It's only been twenty-four fucking hours, man. I'm still breaking in my fugitive shoes. They're in a village two minutes from us. If you were expecting sangfroid, you came up the wrong trail, because I am scared shitless."

Ragnar put a hand on the back of my neck and gave it a squeeze. "They're not going to catch us, brother. Don't forget, we know where they are, but they don't have any idea about us. They're just fishing and got lucky. Yes, they have guns, but we have the mountain, and you are going to guide us out of here."

"Fucking A."

Twenty minutes into Yiorgos's coffee a BMW pulled up in front of the monastery and parked. It was our guys for sure, but they didn't get out of the car right away. They sat there, smoking. Ragnar and I swallowed hard, both of us wondering what these guys knew. Are they following Yiorgos, or did they just drive out here to check it out? It was something they *would* do. It afforded a fabulous view, and you could nip in for a wee bit of prayer if you were so inclined. They got out of the car. There wasn't that much to them, just a couple of hoods, thick, muscled but not imposing. Yet even from this distance they exuded menace and violence. Standing in the gravel lot in the late afternoon sun they turned in place scanning the area. We were above and to the west of them, fortunately, for the sun was already at the ridge behind us. When they looked our way they were looking directly into the sun, and the woods were cast in dark shadow. After several minutes scrutinizing the bush they turned to each other and spoke briefly. Then one of them walked over to Yiorgos's van and glanced inside, he gave the door handle a pull but it was locked, while the other walked over to where Yiorgos was sitting and stood looking north towards Mystras. He pulled out a pack of cigs and then turned and offered Yiorgos one. They too spoke briefly. We were much too far away to hear anything.

I had a terrible knot in my stomach, I wasn't hungry anymore. We were both dead still, breathing as lightly as we could, paralyzed by the scene below us. Our attention was complete. Like an old silent movie yet slower, and the second man came up on the other side of Yiorgos's bench, nodded to him, and stared out at the view. Mostly likely they were searching for sign of us in the sharp valley below.

Our Bulgarians finished their smokes, turned and look at each other, and slowly walked back to their car, all the while scanning the mountain; but the mountain was too big for their eyes, too vast to process, it repulsed their puny needs and held us fast. When they entered the car we exhaled, and followed that by flooding ourselves with oxygen, one deep breath and then another, as they started their car and drove back toward the village. Yiorgos remained, still and cool, a Buddha on the bench, from here he looked dense, immovable, a stone.

He had something in his hand, Ragnar's phone rang, and we both jerked, startled. Rags whispered into the phone, "What the fuck." I could hear Yiorgos, who was not whispering. "Holy shit, that was intense! I thought at one moment, when the second guy walked up, I thought they were just going to grab me and throw me off the cliff."

I took the phone. "Yiorgo my man, I'm really sorry to put you in danger. I had no idea something like this could happen."

"You don't need to apologize, it was exciting as hell. Ten times better than any movie. And I played it cool. Just chilling with the view, sipping my coffee. Smoking his cigarette. I had my ear buds in too but I didn't have any music playing. That way I could pretend I didn't hear them if I wanted to." Ragnar and I exhaled again with relief and exchanged a smile.

"Yiorgo, when he spoke to you, what did he say and in what language?"

"Heavily accented English. 'You want smoke?' And then he said, 'Is beautiful, no?' There wasn't any true suspicion vibe, just my nervous projection. Obviously they're looking for you, but they don't know anything. That's my guess, anyway."

"Yiorgo, you *are* the secret agent, man."

"Where are you guys, anyway?"

"We're about halfway up the hill to the west of you. See the gravel road leading off to your left?"

"Yeah."

"About three hundred meters up that road there's a place you can park that is pretty hidden. We'll meet you there in twenty minutes."

We walked for a couple of hours after loading up Gurdjieff with the supplies and camped on a flat bit among the pines. We made tea from the *tsai tou vounou* we had gathered over the day and had a feast of salami and cheese and paxamadi drizzled with olive oil.

"Rags, I think you should give Yiorgos a cut."

He stared into the small fire we had built. "Yeah, that seems fair enough. I'll take care of him, but first I gotta get out of here, out of Europe. Though, when you think about it, he found his brush with danger so exhilarating that I probably could have charged him."

We laughed together. Yiorgos's account of his encounter with our Bulgarian gangsters conjured up the terrors of the German occupation—the partisans hiding, the SS searching for them. Ragnar grabbed the jug of tsipuro Yiorgos had surprised us with and poured us each a cup. "That was too fucking close today. They're literally right behind us. If we had made any mistakes we would have been fucked. What if Yiorgos hadn't scoped the village out? They'd have had us most likely. We can't expect to do that again. We have to get further ahead."

"Truth that. I should have had Yiorgos bring up some nappies, 'cause I've almost shit myself twice in the past twenty-four hours. But, and maybe I'm just trying to fool myself, I think that this was their chance, and they missed it." I shrugged and held my hands up, then held out my cup. "Mazel tov, comrade."

"Yamas, you lucky bastard." He spit in the fire and was rewarded with a hiss. "The past twenty-four hours have been, dare I say, rather cinematic. I keep expecting the camera crew to step from the bush. Brilliant blue skies above two men far too old to be doing this shit, and a donkey, three dogs, and a crow, all of them with ridiculous pretentious names, making their slow way along the side of a mountain of heaving gray rocks and dark pines. We should be singing songs from 'The Sound of Music.' The hills, my friend, are fucking alive."

"Yeah, but they were fleeing Nazis, whereas we're on the run because you mistakenly ripped off the wrong gangsters."

Ragnar rubbed his chin. "That would appear to be the case." He sang, "How do you solve a problem like the mafia?"

"California is a garden of Eden/it's a paradise to live in or to see/ but believe it or not, you won't find it so hot/ if you ain't got the do-re-mi."

"Oh, deftly played," said Ragnar. "Very nice." We bumped fists and had another drink.

Is your mother still alive?"
     "Nah."

"Mine neither. We're the elders of our clans."

"And obedient to our glands."

"No, no, I'm way too tired for that. Tomorrow while we're walking we can rhyme. Tonight I got no game."

Ragnar tsked, "What a shame."

The next day we made our way south and down into forested alpine valleys back behind the first wave of mountains before the larger thrust of the full range. There was plenty of water, even the last of the snow melt, flooded with crocus and daisy.

"Rags, I'm gonna take you to someone. A very curious, strange character. I'd like to hear what he has to say."

"So, is this the real shaman, the true wise man of the mountains?"

"Maybe."

"And what, he lives up here?"

"Actually, yeah, he does."

"Jesus Christ, Max. Are you trying to drag this out? Why would we be paying some hermit a visit? I thought we were on the lam, escaping, going south?"

"We're safe in the mountains. Eventually those guys will give up. It behooves us, if you will, to take our time, to linger over the crocuses and daisies. When we come down off the mountain, we don't want to be the same people we were when we climbed up."

Ragnar turned and grinned. "Is this the kind of shit you lay on the pilgrims?" He looked down the valley. "Mind you, you do it pretty well. But it is inevitable that we will be different, transformed. And not just because there are two guys who want to kill us hot on our heels. You can't stay the same. None of us can. I was somebody else two days ago."

"Yeah, lying in a hammock reading poetry out loud, like fucking Byron or something."

"We've outlived him by many years, haven't we?"

"Oh, many. He was what, thirty-five or something. Young, but led a full life by all accounts. Shelley died even younger, twenty-nine. They were in Italy at the same time as Keats. Have you been to the Protestant cemetery in Rome?"

"Oh yeah, I have. A shrine of sorts, a holy grotto of poetry."

"Gramsci is buried there too. And Corso! Gregory is buried right next to his favorite poet, Shelley. They don't bury people there anymore, but special dispensation was made for Gregory. That's great, I love it. Just a little stone but enough for a poem he wrote for it. He was really funny, with this just-over-the-top style, demeanor, persona. Damn, hanging out with him in Boulder that summer was great. He had this squeaky, cartoonish Brooklyn accent in which he spoke with an exaggerated flamboyance. Anecdote and confession, erudite considerations of writers, mentorish advice, all sorts of shit, it just flowed out of him in this stream, he was always on. Pure ego, Allen called it. Smoking, drinking, that was something I understood right away, have extra smokes and money to buy the drinks." The memory made me laugh. "He often didn't have *any* money. It was like a badge of honor or something. This meant that he was always on the hustle. For whatever reason, he liked me so we hung out a lot."

"I think it's funny that you refer to him and Ginsberg as Gregory and Allen."

"Well, we got that from them, really. They always used the first name when discussing the other, so we did too. Though Corso was into nicknames, sometimes he said, 'Ginzee.' Oh, and this was at Naropa, right? The big guru there was Chogyam Trungpa Rinpoche, the brilliant, flawed Tibetan lama. Hundreds of devotees meditating away. Gregory called him 'The Chog' or 'The Rimp.' Mostly just to get a reaction from the believers. He loved stirring things up. He trafficked in outrage. Like a child trying to be annoying. Their friendship was a lovely thing to be around. Allen had infinite patience with Gregory. I remember a reading Allen was giving, hundreds in the audience paying rapt attention, and out of the crowd comes that voice, it cuts like a knife, 'Allen, did we ever get it on?' Allen calmly looked up from the poem, 'No, Gregory, we never did.' 'Oh, yeah, I couldn't remember.' And then Allen went on with the reading. It was all cool."

Gurdjieff stopped, so the rest of us did as well. We heard a caw, and Langston alighted on Gurdjieff's saddle. Ragnar and I stood stroking and rubbing Gurdjieff. He loved it and got a blissful look on his face, eyes glazed. On top of Gurdjieff's load Ragnar had fastened a small foldout photovoltaic panel that was charging his phone. We removed it along with the rest, he wandered off to eat some flowers and grass, and we paid attention to the dogs, who gathered around for their strokes.

Ragnar asked with a grin, "Didn't Corso puke on Duchamp's shoes?"

That got me laughing. "Isn't that a wonderful sentence to have in your mouth? 'Didn't Corso puke on Duchamp's shoes?' It's too good. Life beats the shit out of art. You can't make up anything better than that. It was in Paris in the fifties. Allen and Gregory were loaded and went to visit Mr. Marcel. Allen was really into visiting writers wherever he went. He very much promoted the idea of the community of writers and how they should have some kind of solidarity. The dedication in 'Howl' is a promotion for Kerouac and Burroughs and Neil Cassady."

"Puking on Duchamp's shoes is an Artaud gesture, I would think." Ragnar bent over and touched his toes. "Derangement of the senses and all, I mean, what better response to Duchamp than that?"

"Did you know that Artaud's parents were Greeks from Smyrna?" Where had I read that?

"Really?"

"Yeah, I don't know if Greek was a first language or anything."

"The thing that comes to my mind with Artaud is Anaïs Nin's description of that lecture on theatre and the plague he gave. She's there with Henry Miller, and Artaud decides to illustrate his theme by reenacting death by plague. Went on and on till only Miller and Nin were left in the audience. According to her."

"Yeah, wasn't he writhing on the floor?" Our reading

had serious overlaps.

"I believe that was part of it."

"I think most people would go back in time rather than forward, if time travel was available."

"But just for a visit, a lookaround. We've lived through a strange, ripe period of history with all this unprecedented global media/trade/human exchange. No one has ever been able to live as we can now. If I had a choice to exchange with any other time in history, I wouldn't."

"And maybe we're the last who will be able to live this way."

Ragnar looked at me quizzically. "I don't know. I believe our children entertain similar options. They've been able to enjoy the extended childhood that the Western middle class allows the young. You know, you fool around with the bohemian life until your late twenties or so, and then you are confronted with the money thing, and maybe even career and children, that stuff."

"I had the children but couldn't get my mouth around the career. I went through the motions for a few years, but then we escaped to Greece. My father, a bootstraps-poor kid who really worked his way up, couldn't understand my lack of ambition. But really, his was so intense and fruitful that the family could take a generation off."

"Yeah, Max, you are even luckier than most, but I declined career as well. I suppose demographically or whatever, we were supposed to get professional degrees and put our shoulders to the wheel and impact our societies. Especially me. I grew up in Mexico, for fuck sake. It was a scandal that I didn't do the doctor/lawyer/whatever dance. We both had blessed births. Through my mom I had one foot in Europe. It gave me a perspective that my peers there didn't have. There were other ways to live."

"We both refused the destinies our societies and families assumed were ours. And look where it's led. We're on foot in the mountains pursued by men with guns."

Ragnar held up a hand. I slapped it.

L ate afternoon we crested a hill, and in the small valley below stood a small stone house and outbuildings. A narrow dirt trail curled away from it down the valley. "That's Vassili's place. We'll spend the night there."

"Does he know we're coming?"

"No need."

We could hear goat bells that increased in volume as we neared the house. Stein and O'Keeffe raced ahead, and soon we could hear them and other dogs barking, more goat bells, and bellows, shouts, and whistles from a shepherd goading them on. Goats began to exit the woods on a hill behind the house. They were all wearing bells, and their music rolled toward and over us, a liquid sound, water swirling over rock, denser than that. A tall, rangy man wielding a staff and wearing a large straw hat, like something you'd see in Vietnam, stepped out from the wood, raised his hands, and roared, "EEeeeeeeaaaaaaauuuuuuaabb! Gggoooooooooooooaaaaaaahhhh!" The goats were bleating as they entered the corral, the dogs were barking, goat bells ringing, Gurdjieff started braying. It was deafening. I turned and looked at Ragnar. He had the face of a child, he was utterly delighted.

Vassili got the last goat in and closed the gate. He had three dogs as well, and the whole pack had their noses in each other's genitalia like they were long-lost buddies. They were, I suppose. And then Vassili covered the ground with his long, bony stride, and we embraced. After greetings and introductions, Vassili looked up and saw Langston alight on a branch. "Yasou Langston." He turned and looked at the dogs. "They're not all here. Um . . . Voltaire, where's Voltaire?"

"That's the story we bring."

Vassili quickly quieted. "Well come on in. We'll build a fire and have a drink. This way, Ragnar, you are most welcome."

A very rudimentary kitchen was on the front porch, and the cabin was one room with a large wood stove that you could cook with. Bags of herbs hung from the rafters, bird feathers and pine cones from hooks in the wall, totems of the natural world, his life a full immersion in his environment. He had become the language of what he saw. It was very ordered and contained, most everything made from the materials at hand. Shelves attached to the walls held a small but carefully selected library, books that demanded rereading, re-annotating, transcribing yet again into the latest notebook.

Vassili was about ten years older than us, lean, hard, weathered with life on the mountain. Into his fifties he had traveled the world organizing, facilitating resistance to the empire, always the most experienced agitator in the scene. Slightly mad, on occasion infuriatingly doctrinaire, Comrade Vassili invariably wore out his welcome, wherever he went, and would return to Greece to brood and plot and denounce his enemies, both real and ephemeral. Finally he gave it up, he wasn't welcome anywhere, built this cabin on public lands, and began attempting to make sense of it on the page. Hand-written manuscripts were neatly piled on a small desk, but he didn't share them, only the odd poem that concerned shepherding and the mountain, dogs, raptors, and wild boar.

Ragnar and I took turns telling the story, though most of it was Ragnar's. The candles cast the room in gold and shadow, the stove was radiating, as was the tsipuro we were drinking. Vassili was capable of profound attention and carefully followed our narrative, rarely interrupting with a question or request for clarification. When we got to the 'and here we are' part of our tale, he pushed back in his chair and closed his eyes. I got up and stoked the stove while Ragnar stared at Vassili as though new beings would be sprouting from his forehead any moment now. He was enthralled with his presence, that was apparent, but I had the feeling it wasn't going to be reciprocal.

Vassili opened his eyes, leaned forward, put his elbows on his knees, and said, "I saw these men this morning." I started to sputter but V. held up his hand for quiet. "Up above to the west, just out of Rizana. They had parked their car and were standing near it smoking, looking out across the mountains. They were so foreign to the terrain, they might as well have been clad in neon. I was on the motorbike, they didn't pay me any attention. But they were just as you describe them, crude blunt instruments. No one in the Greek countryside would rat you out to those two. They're everyone's worst nightmare. I'm glad I didn't know of the murders of Voltaire and Bukowski, I might have done something, though what that would be I can't say. Given them bad directions, perhaps." He took a good pull of tsipuro and then a drink of water. "So they are convinced that you and Ragnar are on foot in the mountains. And they are close at hand." He pulled a hand through his shaggy grey hair. "You are in no danger here, only a dirt bike or a very rugged four-wheel-drive vehicle can make it, but despite their appearance these men are very resilient and resourceful. Obviously they have obtained maps, have studied them, and are considering the possible routes you may take. And, just as obviously, they are patient, they have done this before. They keep putting themselves in positions where they might get lucky. We can assume they don't know just how close they have missed you. Max, you were right to stay in the mountains. Even with Gurdjieff and the dogs, the chances of them finding you, no matter how lucky and intuitive they may be, is nearly nil, especially as you have stayed away from roads. But I'd guess they are not giving up. And until they do you must be extremely careful."

"What kind of car were they driving?" Ragnar asked.

Vassili swiveled toward him, pointed a finger, and in sharp, clear tones declared, "You, you exotic bird, you have betrayed a friend, a friend you love. And because of that he has betrayed me."

Ragnar recoiled. "What?"

"There is no excuse, a man with your experience carelessly bringing this poison into our lives, into these sacred mountains. No," he held up a hand, "you will shut up and listen. To have lived this long, you must have been better at it once, but now all you are is an old, careless thief. I imagine you tell yourself that you're getting out of the game, ending on a winning note, but you haven't won anything yet, and I wouldn't bet on your chances."

I was mortified and ashamed. "Ah Vassili, I'm sorry, man. These guys just showed up, we had to make a run for it."

"'Just showed up?' Max, please, don't insult me as well. They're here because Ragnar ripped them off and they want it back. And you can't negotiate a settlement for fear they'll kill you anyway. It only ends well if you never encounter these guys, any other narrative would be dire." He turned his head quizzically and looked at Ragnar. "I'm on Max's side, it's his welfare I'm concerned with. But I don't know you. I don't know anything about you; for instance, what you did that these men have pursued you across international borders for fucking days. This looks like vengeance or silencing, like something out of Albania, like their sole purpose is to put a bullet in your head. Maybe everything is as you say, but this is what it looks like. Those guys look like hit men. They'll keep looking as long as the boss wants them to look."

We listened to the wood crack and burn in the stove. Vassili got up and checked the wild greens he had cooking on the stove, opened the door of the oven, and poked at the potatoes he had baking. Vassili was partisan as only a lifelong Marxist-Leninist can be. The first order of business is to take sides, is to choose where you stand and with whom. Neutrality is reactionary. By choosing you define the enemy. I could never consider Ragnar my enemy, but what Vassili had said about betrayal was churning about in my stomach. The more I thought about it, the more likely it seemed that Ragnar wasn't giving us the whole story. I hadn't thought to doubt what he had said. He was my friend telling me what happened. This was why I had come to Vassili, to get his hard sharp view of things, but I hadn't thought that before we came. Maybe enlightenment is knowing why you are doing things when you're doing them. Knowing before you did stuff would be too much.

That would eliminate most surprise. I can move through the world with a degree of comfort because I'm confident that the decisions I'm making will not lead to disaster. I often don't understand why I'm doing things, but I'm not worried about it. One reason is that it only concerns me. No one else is involved. In most all situations in life I'm only responsible for myself. That's a great liberation. This is all predicated on leading a low-key, relaxed life where what's for lunch is a major decision and there isn't a right choice. There are many choices that would bring pleasure. And now I found myself in this fucking adventure movie where a wrong choice could lead to pain, extra suffering, maybe death. It wasn't exciting, it was terrifying. 'Exciting' brings exhilaration, or should, but 'terrifying' brings indigestion, muscle twitches, headache, insomnia. And I was only three days in. I've never harbored any fantasies about combat. It sounds like hell, and every conversation with a war vet has confirmed this. No wonder they were loaded. This shit storm didn't make me want to get high, rather I wanted to fall asleep and dream the thing away.

Vassili placed the spuds and wild greens on the table along with some wild boar he'd smoked and feta and olives. Ragnar and I were ravenous, and we dug in. No one spoke during the meal. Afterward Vassili made us some tea and we put our feet up. I had no idea how Ragnar was taking Vassili's critique. His demeanor revealed nothing. We could hear owls calling.

"Okay, Max," Vassili asked, "what's your plan? How are you going to get these guys off your trail?"

I sighed. "I don't really know. I thought we would continue south, and around the Prophet Elias, Ragnar could head west down to Kardamyli, where he could catch a ride, bus, taxi to Kalamata and the airport. I would continue south to Christos and Eleni's place up above Arna where I would lie low for a few weeks or something. It isn't much of a plan, I know. I didn't realize these guys would be so determined."

"That's my fault," said Ragnar. "I had no respect for these guys. I couldn't imagine they could find me. I still can't figure how they made the connections that led them to Max's hut. I mean, it's all my fault, obviously, and for that I am sorry, for whatever that's worth."

"Not a fuck of a lot." Vassili was all tough love. "Max, if you want to guide your friend out of here, leave the animals with me. You can travel faster and are less conspicuous. And you," he turned to Ragnar, "have to become less visible." He looked Ragnar over and then rose to his feet. "First, take these scissors and cut off that hair. We're about the same size. I'll kit you out in some of my clothes. We want to make you look like a local, a shepherd or something.

Truth is a flexible thing, as is its utility. I didn't really have any choice. I was all in. I was on Ragnar's side no matter what, regardless of his reluctance to be forthcoming. The Bulgarians were convinced that Ragnar and I had escaped into the mountains. It was the only conclusion we could come to given their snooping about. This meant my fate was twined with his. To act without knowing, that felt a more powerful affection than needing to know. A faith, like believing in a god.

Vassili and I both got a good laugh at the result of Ragnar's mirrorless snipping. He looked like badgers had given him a haircut with their teeth. Well chewed. Little blond tuffs sprouted here and there. "Give me those fucking things," I said and finished the job. His shoulder-length dirty blond hair lay on the floor, and he was transformed. Vassili studied him for a moment and then went to a wall where several hats hung off pegs and selected a dark felt hat with a medium brim.

"Greece doesn't have much of a hat tradition. Probably the most popular hat now is the, puke, baseball hat. I don't have one of those. This is a medium gaucho I picked up in Argentina years ago. It won't draw too much attention and will conceal you." He handed it to Ragnar, who turned it in his hands before placing it on his head.

"Wow, you do look different."

"Yeah?" Rags looked up at Vassili. "*Gracias, señor, el sombrero esta muy bien.*"

Vassili shook his head. "*¿De donde diablos eres, hombre?*"

"*México es mi patria, pero vivo en todas partes.*"

"*Chinga tu madre!* Max, where on earth did you find this guy?"

"San Francisco. He had flowers in his hair. It was love at first sight."

We were gathered around the table studying a map by lamp and candle light. "It's pretty straightforward. You'll follow this valley south, and then you'll pick up this other one going west. You could get on a road here at Voreio, or you can continue down the valley all the way to the sea. There's a small road from there up the coast towards Kalamata. You should leave before dawn, I would think."

"Yeah, an early start would be good. If we can make it to about here by noon, then Rags could make it near Voreio by nightfall, and I can make it back here. I've been thinking, I'd like to take the dogs but leave Gurdjieff. They provide an early-warning system."

"Two of them died sounding a warning."

"They did, but we're all endangered here. They are bound to me, so they share it. That's the way it has to be."

Vassili smiled, the solidarity rationale appealed to him, reminded of his struggles down in the world. Ragnar was silent, studying the map. I'd never seen him chastised, admonished so thoroughly. I found it endearing. He had become the 'bad child' he most certainly was in his youth.

He pointed to the valley that ran down toward the Messenian Gulf. "What's the terrain like here?"

Vassili glanced down and pointed at the map. "This dotted line indicates a footpath, so you'll be fine. I haven't taken that route all the way to the sea, but it's Mediterranean alpine forest, dry, not a lot of undergrowth, you'll be able to make good time. The more I think about it I believe it would be wise to avoid the roads and go all the way to the sea here at Akrogiali. Then you could walk this road here at night. That would reduce your exposure. Up here where the small coast road joins the main road is quite developed, and you ll be able to get a cab. We should assume they'll be looking on that side of the mountain as well. They'll probably spend a couple of days driving up and down the coast, from Kalamata to, say, Kardamyli. Sitting at cafés, snooping and waiting."

Ragnar looked up at Vassili. "Thank you, comrade. I realize I don't deserve your help but I really appreciate it."

"Deserve. None of us deserve anything. But we usually get what's coming to us. My friendship with Max means I take him with whatever baggage he brings." Vassili's rough, weathered face looked fierce in the candlelight.

His hard dedication to his own code of honor made him a stalwart companion, but it also caused all groups to finally expel him. The history of revolutions reveals that his type are swiftly executed in the aftermath by the pragmatists.

"I'm going out for a smoke if anyone cares to join me," said Ragnar, standing up. That appealed to Vassili, and I joined them to check on Gurdjieff. The night sky was sharp and vast. Flanked by mountains, we were free of artificial light and high above the humidity clouds in the valley. The lack of moonlight lent the stars a special flashing brilliance. Outside, too, of the mechanical sounds of the world, we stood beneath the star-strewn sky listening to the sound of the mountains at night. How meager we are, how insignificant with our petty adventures, romances, treacheries, desperately attempting to affix meaning to our careening pinball lives. And how wonderful to be in the mix with two close friends beneath 'the starry dynamo in the machinery of night,' solid on the earth and ready for tomorrow.

Vassili exhaled a plume of smoke. "'Hell is empty, all the devils are here.'"

I gave half a laugh. "What play is that?"

"'The Tempest.' First act, Ariel speaking."

"Still reading Shakespeare, huh?"

"I read through the entire works every year."

"Wow. I bow to your discipline and dedication. Or is it mostly about isolation?"

Ragnar added, "'*El ver mucho y el leer mucho avivan los ingenios de los hombres.*'"

I turned to Ragnar. "Huh?"

Vassili cut in. "It's Cervantes. It means that seeing and reading much sharpens one's ingenuity."

"Does that mean we should stay up all night reading?"

Ragnar gripped me by the shoulder. "Tomorrow is about the body, brother. And we will not creep but stride fully toward our fates."

"Amen, I guess."

Vassili's rooster woke us up, and then the smaller birds joined in, like a soft twittering rainfall, flutes and penny whistles. We sat outside his house with tea watching the sky slowly pale. Breakfast was a bowl with a chunk of feta in it, olives and oil, and we mopped it up with paxamadi. We didn't talk much, just let the day settle into us. The dogs walked about performing yoga postures and sniffing the air. I was stroking Gurdjieff's nose. "I'm leaving you here, dude, but don't sweat it. I'll be back by nightfall. I hope."

"Oh, give me a break," laughed Ragnar. "You act like you're about to go into battle." He grabbed a hoe. "Here's your weapon, man. Think of the Bulgarians as weeds."

"Laugh if you will, but I've never claimed to be Dangerman. Nor have I ever wanted to be. Life is dangerous enough without all this, guys with guns hot on our fucking trail. Jesus Christ. I'm comfortable with the regular dangers: cancer, car accidents, lightning strikes, and falling space debris."

"Max, look at the life you've been leading. You've pulled back from everything. Getting sick is the only danger you face."

"So you think it's retreat, my little shaman thing?"

"Hiding, that's what it looks like."

"Huh, I've always thought of it as moving forward, deepening the inquiry. But I see your point. Anyway, the

199

choice has been made for me. That show has closed."

"You can call my arrival an intervention. I'm saving you from yourself."

"By putting my ass in danger. Thank you so goddamn much. Without you I'd still be back chilling at my hut. Hell, I wouldn't even be awake yet."

Vassili gave us each a small bag with a chunk of smoked boar, another of cheese, and some hard-boiled eggs. "You should each take a small bottle of water, but you'll find water along the route. The more you stay down in the canyons and valleys the less visible you are." He took a look at Ragnar in his shepherd getup and laughed. "You look the part, anyway." He glanced up at the brightening sky. "I think you guys should hit it."

We embraced. "Big thanks, Vassili. I'll be back by dark."

Vassili turned to Ragnar, who was hesitant. "Oh, come here, you bastard." They exchanged a hug. "They're driving a black BMW about ten years old."

"*Muchas gracias, mi hermano. No olvidaré.*"

"*De nada.*"

We hiked three hours before stopping for rest and a snack. It was sunny but not too hot, the mountains were glorious. The dogs were loving it.

"Remember that time we got lost in Yosemite?" Ragnar asked.

"I don't think I'll ever forget that, but it was Kings Canyon. You threw the I Ching to determine the way out. And it worked!"

"Of course it worked, but really, it was the flight of birds I was reading. It is the energy of the practitioner that speaks through the random cast, that colors the divination, that brings the ancient wisdoms into the present."

"You are so full of shit."

"Yeah, but so is everyone else. It all boils down to style and panache."

"Panache?"

"That's right. Verve, daring, chutzpah."

"You're not going to tell me what you really did in Bulgaria, are you?"

Ragnar looked off down the valley and then turned to me and smiled. "No, I'm not. And it's not to avoid your disapproval, 'cause really, your disapproval is a given, even if you don't express it. I'm going to keep this one to myself. I don't want to hear myself describe it. Maybe it's *my* disapproval I avoid, as though not saying it out loud leaves it vague, not quite in focus, just an idea."

"So maybe these guys chasing us merely want to argue theory and analysis?"

"If only." Ragnar pulled out his phone and looked at it. "What time is it?"

"Only 9:30. I'm waiting for when I can get a signal. The mountains are blocking it."

"You need to make a call?"

"I just had a thought, and it gave me chill. I should have thought of it right away. If these guys can find out about you and your hut in the mountains and make the connection with me, they won't have any problem tracking down Luciana in Barcelona."

A shiver ran through me. "Oh fuck. What are you going to do?"

"I'm going to call her and tell her to get on the next plane to Copenhagen. She can stay with some friends

201

there, not her relatives. This will give her an extra layer of anonymity."

"Jesus. And she'll do that?"

"It might take a little convincing, but I think so. She'll probably bargain with me. I'll have to pay her off. That's the fate of the absent parent, always negotiating from a weak position."

"Where's Jeanne Marie?"

"She's back in Montreal. That is one of Luciana's standard gambits, she's going to tell her mother. I'd rather face the Bulgarians than the rage of Jeanne Marie. And I would deserve it. But who the fuck wants what they deserve? We want what we desire. Fortunately, there isn't such a thing as an international restraining order, otherwise I'd already be operating under it. And we've been divorced for more than ten fucking years."

"You've never struck me as marriage material."

"I am decidedly not. The whole thing was a disaster. Luciana was the only positive outcome of it. And I fucked that up too. Your attention is the greatest gift you can give them, it's what they want, and I was not very generous. I was on the go too much, or when I was around was up all night and slept all day. This is not a recipe for good parenting."

"Yeah, okay, you were a shitty parent. It's done. You can't go back and re-parent. I haven't seen her for years, but I never got the impression that Luciana was severely damaged by your neglect. She's a nice person, she'll do well. Jeanne Marie did a great job. You'd like to feel better about yourself, I get it. So be there for her now, that's all you can do. That, and stop doing things that put others in danger."

Ragnar turned and gave me half a smile. "Ah so, this is what you do. You slap 'em in the face and tell 'em to clean up their mess." He put his hands together in a *namaste* gesture, bowed his head ever so slightly, and in a faux-Asian accent, "So very much in your debt, master."

We both stared off down the valley full of pine and wildflower. Two eagles scribed slow circles as they worked their way south. Their cries echoed up to us. They appeared, as they often did, far too high to see or strike prey, the sky a hard, aching blue. Without turning, Ragnar said, "Do not quote Yeats."

"Okay. Things will fall apart regardless of whether we mark it with po."

"They already have, I feel like Humpty Dumpty. Where oh where are all the king's horses? Remember the opening of *All the King's Men*?"

"The heat, the hypnotic highway, maybe you'll crash. I love that opening. 'Another one done hit.' Good book. I've never read anything else of his. I couldn't bear his po. But that's a great opening. Right up there with *A Farewell to Arms*."

"You think it's *that* good?"

"Maybe not. I'm not sure what is. The cadence, those single-syllable words, the way they echo the sounds of boots marching on the road. The ominous mood. Hemingway was doing what no one else had. Ninety years later we're still thinking about it."

"Tell me, Max. Illustrate how I should have raised my child. I've always entertained the illusion that you were the model parent."

"Oh, gimme a fucking break. Everything about our situations was different. Though truth be told, the first five years of my kids' lives I wasn't around that much. I was working all the time running those bullshit bars. But when we moved to Greece everything changed. Then Briseis was the one working, and I became the primary caregiver: cooking the meals, doing the laundry, driving them around, handing out money, you know, doing all the mundane stuff so they could get on with living life, responsible only to themselves—a luxury, perhaps, but a good one when you're inventing yourself. We insisted on them making their own decisions, for instance, whether to go to school. We were this isolated family unit in a tiny village in the Greek countryside. We never had a TV so we entertained ourselves. We were together every day. Before we had the kids I wasn't particularly into children, but everything changed when they arrived. Then I was intensely interested in everything about them. I wonder what it would have been like if they had been dull, slow to pick things up, rather than the whiz kids they were. And then, when they were teenagers, Briseis was in full decline, sicker by the year. She just didn't have much energy to give them. She was in and out of hospitals in Athens, and the kids stayed at home alone. But they had each other, they always had that strong, almost mystical connection that twins often have. They've been together since before they were born. And you know, it was funny, not at the time, when the inevitable teenage rebellion came, their mother and I didn't have the time and energy to pay much attention to it. We couldn't take it seriously, which they found very annoying. If you're going to rebel, you want to meet a bit of resistance. The Greek countryside is a great place to have kids, very soft and safe. Sure, in high school they were getting drunk and stoned and having sex, but why not? They connected with different parts of me, they stretched me out and made me more than before. Kids demand that you focus, and they catch every hypocrisy. What they're doing with their lives now feels inevitable, Maki making art and Leo in law school. And in the States. Anyone who can leave does."

"How often do you talk on the phone with them?"

"Not too often. They're very independent, and I'm not much of a phone guy. We email, especially Leo and I, whereas Maki wants more phone. She wants to connect emotionally. I only got back from the States a week ago. I thought I was going to relax at the hut, listen to the odd story, spend some serious time in the hammock. Instead . . ."

"It was time for a change, I'm happy to provide the spark."

"Oh fuck, man, why didn't you just leave me in the dark."

"You know me, I gots to leave my mark."

"Yeah, but this hardly amounts to a walk in the park."

"So sorry, but hark, is that your pack that barks?"

That was my dogs, and we looked down the valley where they were aggressively raising a ruckus. The sharp report of it echoed up toward us magnifying the noise.

"Oh, look, it's a boar." I pointed toward a large, hulking creature moving through chaparral, ignoring the dogs.

"Fuck, that thing is big."

"Yeah, there's no predators, save man, so they get huge. Note that the dogs don't get very close. Vassili kills one a year. It's legal to hunt them, otherwise they would overrun the landscape."

"Like man."

"*Homo homini lupus.*"

Ragnar turned and nodded. "Bravo, we are sharp this morning. 'Man is wolf to man,' still true, if not more so."

"We're the sheep in this equation, aren't we?"

"Bbbaaaaaaaaaaaaahhh."

About noon we reached a place where Ragnar got adequate signal on his phone, and he called his daughter. I walked off with the dogs, who had just returned, to give him privacy, though the call was conducted in Spanish so there wasn't any need. It sounded like pleading to me.

Ragnar looked shaken when he finished the call. He walked up to us shaking his head.

"I hesitate to ask," I said.

"Luciana said she never wanted to see me or speak with me ever again and cursed my name in no uncertain terms."

"Ouch."

"But she is going to fly to Copenhagen tomorrow night. She'll continue her studies online. She was furious and is, more than likely, on the phone to her mother as we speak. I didn't believe my standing with the women in my family could get any worse, but here we are, and I have sunk even lower. They'll probably stop using my name and replace it with some derogatory term, *el pendejo* or the like. Maybe they switched years ago. Luciana has always been firmly in the Jeanne Marie camp."

"Probably because you were an absent, philandering kind of husband/father."

Ragnar gave me an "Et tu, Brute" look. "I see, you're with them too."

I gave an exaggerated look around. "Far as I can tell, I'm with you. I'll always be with you, but that doesn't mean I forget the way you've treated your women. You gotta admit, you deserve it all."

"Again with the fucking deserve. It's like some karmic bullshit ricochet."

"Forget all the reincarnation crap. All karma means is that if you plant an oak seed, you'll get an oak tree, not an apple. It's cause and effect. And with personal relationships it seems unerringly accurate. You know, sow and reap."

He gave a sigh and took off his hat and scratched his freshly shorn head. "So that's it, huh? I'm an unredeemable bastard, despised by all, cursed by the hatred of his family, fucking doomed to die a lonely miserable death in some South American backwater, swatting flies and begging for an opiate."

"Like something out of Graham Greene, only in his version you'd be asking for a priest."

We had a short laugh.

"The only way I'd convert is if that priest had a syringe full of morphine. Hail Morphine, full of grace, my pain is my need. Blessèd are thou amongst drugs, and blessèd is the fruit of holy opium. Not much to look forward to."

"Well, it's not guaranteed. There are many paths from here. I'm not sure how much I believe in free will, but that's all we have to work with. Believing your choices are consciously generated sharpens your focus and, I believe, allows you to invest more in them—even if, in the grand scheme of biological imperatives, they are meaningless. Follow the path that makes you feel better—might be prayer, might be buggery. I don't know. Working with wood, growing the perfect radish, accumulating the most money possible, what-the-fuck-ever. I realize that in this I'm pitching a 'free will' narrative, but fuck it, choose your fantasy, avoid pain and the giving of pain." I shrugged and turned my palms to the sky.

We were standing there amidst the dogs. Ragner had a sly smile on his face and said, "You've been practicing, haven't you."

"All life is practice, and then the game never happens."

"I now regret bringing the curtain down on your shaman thing. It's really sharpened your shtick."

"Everybody has the same problems, really. Generally they're afraid, for any number of reasons, but that's the core. Though I wouldn't say that about you, unless your relationship with Luciana is now based on fear. Fear of rejection, fear of loneliness, fear of being adrift here in the middle of your life."

"'And the straight path was lost.'"

"Okay, but his wife was nuts, whereas yours was intensely sane."

"That's one way to put it. Though only if you're talking about Eliot. Dante had an arranged marriage and several children."

"But spent his life pining for Beatrice."

"Apparently. We don't know much about the wife, but the marriage was arranged before they reached puberty, so the union probably wasn't about romantic love."

"That's a subject for another time. Let's hit it. I'm going to have to turn back pretty soon or I won't make it back to Vassili's in daylight."

We were on the footpath and made good time through the interlocking valleys till we came to where the valley turned due west and followed the Avouros River, and we stopped to eat and rest.

"This is where we part, I would imagine," said Ragnar.

"Yeah, this is good. You just head west from here. It's a pretty straight shot. I don't think you'll be able to get to the sea today, but tomorrow you'll get there in the morning. And from there, catching a cab, you could be at the Kalamata airport in the early afternoon. I agree with Vassili, you should avoid the roads until you can't."

Ragnar reached over and grabbed me by the back of the neck and squeezed. "You did it. I knew you'd get me out of these mountains."

"Without Yiorgos and Vassili it would have been a rough go. We'd be really hungry by now."

"But that's part of you. You know these people, and they leapt to it when you needed them. I'm not surprised, but still, you have not wasted your time in these mountains."

"Wasted? No, and I'm glad that whatever I've achieved up here exists only in the air and memory. I have nothing to show for it, and that was the idea."

"That's all very nice and Taoist, my friend, but now you're going to write it down, aren't you? You're going to turn it into stories."

Now that it was over I had been thinking that it was time to tell the stories, give some form to what I had been given, some celebration of people's generosity. "I've been thinking about that. Once I'm sure the bad guys have left the area, I'll return to the house and see what I can make of it."

"Ha ha, when I arrived you told me my story wouldn't make the cut."

"Wrong again. I prefer situations where there are many options and none of them can be called right or wrong. Whatever happens is okay. But you added the element of danger, and that changed everything."

"Back to fear, aren't we? It certainly got us up and moving."

"The threat of pain and death does that, though truth be told, this was a first time for me. I've never been pursued with murderous intent. And I could have easily lived without it. My whole being was shaking, inside and out, and it would be now if I thought those guys could catch us here. There's a dirt road up on this ridge, but we can't see it so I think we can assume we aren't visible from it." We both scanned the hillside above us, nothing but the stillness of midday. Faint buzzing of insects, a few notes of birdsong. From where we stood there was no sign of man, nothing but the mountain, pine, rock, and the flowers that somehow grew out of the cracks in the rock. We stood silently, knowing it was time to part, both of us wanting to avoid undue expressions of emotion. We both kicked at the loose rock at our feet, noticed that we were both doing it, and had a laugh. We embraced and held it. And then Ragnar hoisted his pack.

"Thank you, brother, I am in your debt." He let his indigo eyes loose.

"I'm glad I could help. It's always great to see you, my friend, but please, don't come if you're on the run. I don't need that much excitement."

"I'll bear that mind. I'll send you word when I get somewhere safe."

"Do that. Be careful. *Kalo taxidi.*"

Ragnar turned and headed off down the path. The dogs started following but stopped when they noticed I hadn't moved. Langston soared after, something in Ragnar spoke to crow. I watched him until he disappeared in the trees.

I was sorry to see him go. We delighted in each other's company, we always made each other laugh. I don't know how many friends Ragnar has, but I know I am one. And for me that feels like a rare and exquisite gift, something that cannot be valued. For me he provides a test, an assessment of where I am in the world, a check on the vanities that tend to creep into your life without notice until the patina of self-regard colors everything. We all need old, fearless friends, those with a depth of mutual experience that sweeps away all pretense, that cares not about what you've become, that core love that insists on naked expression, that still has your twenty-five-year-old persona in their heart.

Some rise by sin, some by virtue fall." That's what Vassili had said the night before. Above me to the north was Tragovouni, He-goat Mountain, where according to legend the male goats would hang out until it was tupping time. I felt I was walking out of danger as I hiked back to Vassili's, as though Ragnar was the scapegoat of the tribe bearing away the curse. The word tragedy in Greek literally means song of the goat, though I've never heard anything out of a goat that resembles song.

I settled in at Vassili's, the two hermits trying to stay out of each other's way, which was simple enough as Vassili took the goats out in the morning and didn't return until late afternoon. Derrida and O'Keeffe went along, pretending they were shepherd dogs, but the ever-loyal Stein stayed behind with me. Langston showed up after a day.

Vassili produced all his own food save sugar, salt, and flour. In the winter he came down for the olive harvest and secured his oil for the year. We very much enjoyed each other's company in the evening by the warmth of the stove.

He didn't get visitors as I had so he had a lot to say, and I kicked back in the easy chair and listened.

A week into my sabbatical Vassili returned on his motorbike with a postcard mailed from Manchester of the Queen waving from a horse-drawn carriage.

Max, Vassili — I let the
Bulgarian swine see me at
last moment at Kalamata   Vassilis Skiadas
airport. You're in the clear,   Artemesia 23410
so am I. Muchas gracias,   Greece
mis hermanos.   Rags

The next morning I loaded up Gurdjieff with supplies, said a brief, emotional goodbye with Vassili, and hit the trail back to my house on the other side of the mountains. It would take two days, but I had plenty of food and water, and the weather was fine. The animals knew we were headed home. I had to pick up my pace to keep up with them. Langston would fly a few minutes ahead and then perch on a tree and wait for us, cawing and calling. I followed my ass, who once again demonstrated that he could walk and shit at the same time.

Lightning Source UK Ltd.
Milton Keynes UK
UKHW011014270919
350576UK00001B/75/P

9 780998 279343